RELEASE

A COLLECTION OF SHORT & SEXY CRAZY
BEAUTIFUL LOVE STORIES

JOLIE MOORE

JOLIE MOORE

This edition published in the United States of America by:

Moore Digital Media Inc

www.joliemoore.com

Copyright © 2021 by Jolie Moore

eISBN: 978-1-64414-043-7
ISBN: 978-1-64414-044-4

Cover Designer: Qamber Designs

(*first published 2015-2018 by Jinni Black*)

Cynthia

Cynthia is in for the ride of her life.

Cynthia needs to forget the guy who dumped her. One plane ticket and a rail pass through Europe should do the trick. Shaking off the past and the prude she used to be is hard until Cynthia meets a certain train conductor who wants make sure she's one hundred percent satisfied with her ride.

ONE

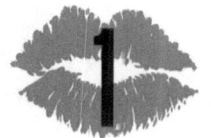

"I DON'T LOVE YOU ANYMORE," Scott said, shifting from foot to foot. The sound the bottoms of his tasseled loafers made against the floorboards was driving her nuts. Cynthia Patterson wanted to tell him to stand still. Stand like a man while he shattered her life into a million tiny pieces. But she remained quiet, like she always did.

Fingernails jagged with stress dug into the flesh of her palms with every movement of his body, every squeak against the floor boards.

"That's it?" she asked of her boyfriend . . . hell, fiancé.

"I took the liberty of packing and moving my stuff out," Scott said.

Liberty? Did he think he'd done her a favor? She let her purse slip from her shoulder. It hit the floor with a soft thump. Cynthia looked around the apartment she and Scott had shared for more than five years. It took a minute to cotton to the fact that something was different about their home.

Then it hit her.

The seventy-five inch flat screen she hadn't wanted in the first damned place was missing from above the electric fireplace. Unconnected wires splayed from a hole in the wall. Of course her regular sized, normal person TV wasn't back to replace it. He'd kindly left that heavy electronic brick in storage in the basement for her to haul up on her own.

She took a deep breath, refocused her eyes elsewhere. The DVD shelf was half empty. Pastel chick flick covers were all that remained. She didn't check to see if he'd left her full set of *Sex and the City* DVDs. No question he'd happily abandoned those. Scott had hated the Cosmo-drinking, self-assured women in that show. He liked his women quiet. She'd tried to be that woman. But it was looking like she'd failed at saying nothing.

Without uttering a word, Cynthia stalked from the living room down the small hallway to the bedroom. Drawers laid open, bare as the day they were delivered from the furniture shop.

She backed out, dry-eyed. She would not cry or turn into a needy, clingy girlfriend. Not now. Not until she assessed what was going on. The second bedroom they'd used as an office looked bare. A shiny dust-free spot was where Scott's computer had been. Wire spaghetti was missing from the floor. In Scott's urge to get 'his' stuff out, he hadn't done anything about the piles of dust bunnies left behind.

When she got back to the living room, finally ready to speak up and demand an explanation, Scott hefted a duffle bag on his shoulder. Probably held the last of his clothes. He looked ready to leave, not talk. Nope, he wasn't getting off that easy. Not this time.

"When did you do all this?" she asked, gesturing toward the naked wall and half-empty shelves.

"This morning." He shrugged, half turning away.

"Didn't your boss wonder why you weren't at work?" He had a great job, but a boss from hell. That guy monitored Scott's comings, goings, and bathroom time. Maybe she should have urged him to quit his job. Maybe that would have made him happier. Made him stay.

"I gave my two week notice," he said.

Well, that wasn't it. He'd thrown off that yoke. "When?"

"Two weeks ago."

Cynthia gripped one hand with the other to stop the shaking. To stop her from hauling off and slapping him. Anger replaced sympathy. She wasn't even deserving of the common courtesy of getting two weeks' notice? Late afternoon sun peeked through the blinds. The rays caught her ring and a burst of multi-faceted light filled the room.

Mesmerized, Cynthia watched the light play on the ceiling.

Scott cleared his throat. "Can I have that?"

"You want the ring back?" she asked, unable to keep the disbelief from her voice. Scott hadn't asked for the platinum and diamond band back when he'd lifted her nightgown and began pounding into her this morning from behind without so much as a kiss or a cuddle. First no foreplay, then no warning.

She closed her eyes, shook her head. Maybe this was a bad dream. She pinched her wrist. The skin turned white, then pinked up again. But she didn't wake up in their . . . in *her* bed. They were both standing right there, shuffling around each other like first round boxers in the ring.

"I'm still paying on it. I need the money for my new place," he said matter-of-factly as if their relationship had been no more than a bank transaction.

"Where are you moving?" If he moved to Providence, far from their place in Smithfield, maybe she wouldn't run into him so often.

"New York City. Brooklyn, to be exact."

Cynthia maybe needed her ears checked. She was sure he was going to say College Hill. He's always aspired to live over that way. The converted mill loft she'd loved in Smithfield had been a compromise. She'd wanted to save money for a wedding and a house. Stay close to her family.

He'd moaned about missing the bar-fueled nightlife

they'd had in college. Over the last few years, he'd never let her forget that he'd deigned to live way out in Smith-field. But New York City was a whole different kettle of fish. He wasn't just dumping her, but their entire lifestyle as well. She watched him. Scott was full of clear-eyed determination. But he didn't seem to remember that Smithfield had been her second choice. With his good-paying insurance company job, he'd refused to leave Rhode Island.

"You didn't want to go to New York after graduation. I begged you. Why now?" Why can't we go together, she wanted to ask. But whiny, needy girlfriend had never been her thing. She'd always stepped back. Kept her distance where he was involved. He'd always hated high-mainte-nance women.

Had he wanted whiny and needy—high-maintenance? Was she too aloof, self-sustained? It took all her willpower not to drop to the floor and beg him like Effie in *Dreamgirls*. But she didn't want to go out like that. Instead, she pushed her hair behind her ear and straightened her spine, telegraphing her pain. Maybe he'd read the signals and capitulate, drop whatever fanciful notion he'd gotten into his head.

Scott didn't say anything for a long while. If he was ready to go, then damn him. Cynthia twisted the diamond ring around her finger a few times until it came off over the knuckle. It flew into a corner of the room behind the couch. That spurred Scott into action. He dropped the duffle and crawled behind the couch on hands and knees.

"Got it," he announced, holding up the precious gem —triumphant.

His bag buzzed loudly, filling the silent vacuum he'd already left. She removed the ringing phone from the uppermost pocket. A number flashed upon the screen. The 718 area code was unfamiliar. Out of habit, she lifted his phone to her ear.

"This is Scott's phone, how can I help you?" Cynthia asked, sounding like she was in customer service and not breakup hell.

"This is Ellen Stephenson," an unfamiliar voice answered. "Scott's fiancé? Can you put him on? I need to give him some directions for the moving truck."

In the single biggest act of defiance in all of her twenty-six years, Cynthia lifted her arm as high as it would reach and let go. The phone dropped nearly six feet onto the scarred wood. The refinished floors that bore the marks of decades of working men and women had been one of her favorite features of the place. But the floors weren't built for living. They were anything but soft. The shiny new iPhone for which Scott had stood in line for six hours was in some big and some little pieces. She gingerly stepped over them, went to the bedroom and slammed the door. He could show himself out.

TWO

THE KNOCK on the door spurred hope and dread in equal measure. She half hoped it was Scott coming to beg for her to take him back. She'd had about a dozen of those fantasies in the last few weeks.

In half of them, they'd kissed and made up. The other half, she'd kicked him in the nuts and sent her ex-fiancée on his way. But she hadn't heard a single word from him since he'd scooped up his phone's guts and stomped out of their apartment. Ellen was no doubt keeping him warm where she couldn't.

The knock came again. She paid closer attention this time. Dread kicked hope to the curb. It was her stepsister Camilla. The rat-a-tat-tat of knuckles against wood was as distinctive as a calling card. Cynthia lifted the pillow she'd been cuddling in her lap, her butt from the couch, and pulled open the heavy wood door ready for the pep talk/ass kicking that Camilla would dole out.

"Are you going to change your clothes and leave the house?" Camilla asked. I don't think she'd ever used the word 'hello.' Since they'd moved in together as kids, she'd wake up and run a hundred miles an hour until she fell into bed and passed out from sheer exhaustion. Cynthia didn't have Camilla's energy or zest for life. Her plan had been to marry her college sweetheart. Buy a house. Have a few kids. Maybe a dog. Grow old together. Everything from the regular menu.

"I plan to wallow a few more months," Cynthia said. The future had gone from a certainty to a big gaping hole of possibilities. None of which she was ready to face.

"You should move on," Camilla said.

"What does that mean—move on? My fiancé up and left me for another woman. How do you suggest I move on from that?" Cynthia couldn't believe what she was hearing from her stepsister. Camilla was platitude central all of a sudden.

Her stepsister released a long sigh. "I mean fuck another guy. A new penis will make you forget about the old one. It's always worked for me."

"Like when?" Camilla was no stranger to 'moving on' all over Smithfield, Providence, and all of Rhode Island, for that matter. But she couldn't believe a penis worked magic like lifting and waving a big, sparkly wand.

"Remember when Tony dumped me?"

Cynthia nodded. Tony had been a piece of work. Camilla had done everything for him from his term papers to his laundry. But he'd left her apartment one morning with a bag of clean and folded clothes and had never come back. Maybe it was a Patterson stepsister's curse.

Camilla didn't wait for any more of a response. "That night I went to a party at Alpha Ro."

"After you graduated?" Even for Camilla, that smacked of desperation.

"That's beside the point. I wanted free booze and a good time," Camilla said.

Cynthia's interest kept her from doing the elaborate eye-roll thing. "What happened?"

"I had a couple of Twisted Lemonades."

"Wait. Is this the party that served drinks from an out-of-commission urinal?"

Camilla nodded. "I told you that part. Now I'll tell you the rest."

Cynthia sat back. She never knew what was going to come out of Camilla's mouth. Might as well grab the pillow and hang on for the ride. "Go on."

"There were two guys who were dancing with me all night. One was bumping and grinding me from the front. The other, the back."

"Did you get their names?"

Camilla looked at Cynthia like she'd half lost her mind. "Let's call them Desmond and Billy."

Names were going to be beside the point in this tale. "Fine. Tell me about Desmond and Billy."

"So we're dancing to Li'l Wayne's 'Lollipop,'" she said.

Cynthia could hear the heavy bass bump and grind in her mind. The dim lights. Two hunky guys dancing like sex on legs.

"Desmond asks me to go back to his room. Billy asks the same. In my head I flipped a coin and picked Desmond because I'd heard good things about his skills around campus."

"Fifth year senior?"

Camilla nodded. "Five and a half. In his case, that was a good thing. He'd had time to perfect his technique."

"Not at education." I crossed my arms and sat back, trying to be a good listener less stick-in-the-mud.

"An-y-way, I walked halfway up the stairs and crooked my finger at Desmond. Like a puppy, he followed me to the top. Then he led me to his room. Because of his seniority, he had a huge room and a king-sized bed. And he was good. Not shy at all and not quick about it. He made sure I was nice and wet before he pulled out his magnificent cock."

Cynthia was nice and wet and slightly horrified that the tale had her turned on. She was a straight up missionary girl—except when Scott took his pleasure. But to voluntarily go and do it with a guy she'd never met. Geez. She took a deep breath. Camilla was still talking. Wasn't sure what she'd missed. "...was like he could go on for hours. I think I'd come two times before he finally let himself go. I wasn't thinking a lick about Tony."

"Okay. Well, I don't know if I can do the random hookup."

Camilla leaned closer, her voice conspiratorial. "Here's what really made me forget about Tony.

I got dressed, ready to join up with the party again, but before I could get downstairs, I heard someone going 'psssst' and calling my name. So I turned left instead of right, following the voice. And there was Billy. His head was sticking out of the door of his room and I followed him into another room."

"'I heard you getting fucked in the other room,' he'd said. "I like a buttered bun. C'mere.'"

"What's a buttered bun?" Cynthia asked. Then stopped.

Oh, shit.

It didn't take a genius, or five and a half years of college to figure that one out. "Did you go in there with him? You'd just..."

"Women are capable of multiple orgasms for a reason."

"Is this a biology lesson?" Cynthia asked.

She knew she should have been disgusted, not turned

on. Leaning forward, she eagerly waited for the rest of the story.

"Not hardly. I went in there. Desmond was long. Billy was thick. It filled me like..." Camilla's eyes practically rolled back in her head. "Let's just say he hit my g-spot."

Now Cynthia *had* to roll her eyes. "Is that for real? Seems as mythical as the Bermuda triangle."

Camilla nodded. "It's as real as Amelia Earhart's plane."

"So, Tony?"

"Who?" Camilla said. Cynthia had to laugh at that. After that tale, *she* barely remembered Tony. She may never think of Tony again. Desmond and Billy, on the other hand, had seared a permanent place in her memory. Maybe one day she'd be that kind of woman. She shook her head. Cynthia wasn't that kind of woman. She was a big believer in serial monogamy. It would be a long time before she took the plunge again.

THREE

CYNTHIA SAT in her mother and Camilla's father's kitchen, letting the sun warm her and the draft raise goose bumps. She sipped at ginger tea and watched her blended family bustle around the butcher block-topped island. They were centered around Camilla who was doing something crazy with a hand-held blender. Buzz. Buzz it went.

Ten minutes later, Camilla came to the oak table with mousse in hand. Cynthia dipped in the spoon Mom had given her into the lemon yellow foam. The pineapple concoction was tart, sweet . . . surprisingly good.

"I'm taking a sabbatical," she announced in between licks of the spoon.

"Like a professor?" Camilla's dad Roy asked. "You're not a professor."

She was aware that her job in marketing at a company that managed state lottery systems wasn't as glamorous as academia. But for employees with five years or more of solid service, her company offered the opportunity to take six months off with half-pay. When the memo landed in Cynthia's e-mail inbox last Monday morning, she hit reply as fast as her hands could type.

There in her lap had landed the single best excuse to get the hell out of Rhode Island, the hell out of America, in fact. Two hours after that first e-mail, she found herself snaking through the corridors to Human Resources, signing documents and handing over her duties to an eager wet-behind-the-ears college graduate.

"What are you going to do?" her mom asked. She'd put down her own dessert spoon and was nervously twisting one hand around the other. Cynthia looked into her mom's blue eyes. They looked wide with panic. You'd think she just announced she was sky-diving, not taking time off a boring marketing job.

Cynthia took a deep breath. "I'm backpacking through Europe," she announced.

"Way to go!" Camilla whooped, high-fiving her. Cynthia's hand awkwardly missed her stepsister's. The downside of not being the cool one.

"Where are you going to stay?" her mother asked. This time Mom had picked up the dishtowel and was twisting it in her hands. Mesmerized, Cynthia watched the blue striped waffle fabric move between her fingers.

Cynthia pulled a small laminated card from the purse at her side and slid it across the table. "Hostels."

Roy plucked the card from the wood. "Aren't you too old for this?"

Maybe Scott had left her because she was old and unadventurous. Her family surely treated her that way. "Not at twenty-six. I probably should have done this trip when I was out of school. But I did the predictable thing and got a job."

"You don't have to do this just because of Scott," her mother said. "I'd be happy to spend the time with you. I could take you to the garden club. You could help me with the Friends of the Library fundraiser."

Cynthia certainly didn't say it. But that would be her idea of hell. Suddenly traveling alone didn't seem as daunting as it had a few days ago when she'd hatched the scheme. "I want to do this. I want to see the world. I bought a Eurail pass," she said.

"By yourself?" Her stepfather sat back. His salt and pepper curls glinted in the sun. Absently she wondered if her hair would look like that in a quarter-century. If it did, Cynthia wanted to travel while she was still young and it was still easy to hoist a full backpack and lug it around.

"I've bought a three-month pass." She'd emptied her savings for that two thousand dollar ticket. "Airline seats too. I'm flying into London next Saturday."

"What about your apartment?" her stepdad asked.

"Sublet," she answered quickly before her family could spread seeds of doubt.

"You've covered all your bases," Camilla said, nodding approvingly. "Did you buy one of those honking medal frame backpacks?"

Cynthia nodded. "It's out in the vestibule," she said, getting up to bring it in for show and tell.

Roy checked the frame and closures, pronouncing it safe. With their tacit approval, and promise to put her car and personal belongings in storage, Cynthia was practically on her way.

FOUR

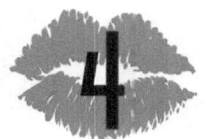

ALONG WITH HER brand new hiking shoes and iPad, Cynthia laid the new Java red backpack on the conveyor belt. Security in New York City, where she was connecting through to London, was more serious than the single terminal airport in Providence. Men with big guns and little dogs roamed the corridors.

After holding her hands over her head and being pelted with radiation, she stood on the other end of the conveyor belt, looking for her stuff to emerge. Bouncing in her socks, Cynthia waited for her backpack. Every single thing she needed for the six month trip was in there. No way she could leave it behind. It went in and out of the scanner, not three but four times.

"Miss." A TSA officer waved her over. "Over here. We need to do an extra search."

Dutifully, Cynthia followed the guy over. Another

blue uniformed guy joined the first with her bag in one hand and the bin carrying her shoes and tablet in another. Standing in the cordoned-off area with her feet planted a foot apart, she waited for a woman with a wand to appear. "Is a female officer coming?" she asked.

The guys looked at each other, then her. "We can handle this," the blond one said. A little shiver ran through her when Cynthia's eyes met his. It was the first time she'd been attracted to anyone since Scott had walked out the door. Turning her head, she gave the full-bearded dark-haired guy standing legs wide, hands on his hips in classic cop stance, the once over. He wasn't too bad either. Most of her friends weren't a fan of facial hair, but Cynthia thought it could be kind of sexy. A brief picture of that soft hair brushing between her thighs caused heat to steal up her spine.

"We need to open your backpack," the dark-haired one said, cutting her fantasy short. "There's something buzzing in there."

"Do you have a phone?" the blond asked.

She shook her head. "No phone." Cynthia had planned to buy a cheap throwaway compatible with Europe's systems.

"Any other electronics? Weapons?"

"Nope. Going on vacation. Just the iPad here," she said, gesturing to the bin. "Can I put on my shoes?" It was weird cooling her heels in her old hiking socks from college. Cynthia felt kind of vulnerable. She curled her toes. Air hit her left big toe. She looked at the sock. Damn, there it was, a hole. A pink painted toenail wiggled back and forth free from the wool.

"Can we open the pack?"

Cynthia threw her head back in exasperation. It had taken her a couple of days to figure out how to roll her clothes and fit all of them in there. The jeans were jammed in pretty hard this morning. Underwear, the smallest items, topped the lot.

"Fine." If they wanted to see her panties, so be it.

They pulled at the metal frame and her red backpack slid along an aluminum table. It was then she heard the faint buzzing as well. It was like a kitchen timer was shoved deep in the recesses of her bag.

Camilla had said something about leaving her a surprise. But her stepsister wouldn't leave a timer in there. Not in today's world where it sounded like a ticking bomb. Suddenly, she was nearly as alarmed as the officers. Please, she prayed, let the sock hole be the most embarrassing thing to happen today. Please let Camilla not have done something stupid that would land her in federal lock-up on this side of the Atlantic Ocean.

Cynthia watched as they pulled first underwear, then jeans, then t-shirts from her bag. Her windbreaker came next. It was balled up in a haphazard way she didn't remember doing herself. The dark-haired TSA agent unrolled it and the culprit popped out, buzzing on the heap of clothing.

Shit. Shit. Shit. She was going to kill Camilla.

Yesterday, her stepsister had offered to do the driving, taking her shopping for last minute items Cynthia had forgotten. She'd already put her own car in storage in her parent's garage and didn't want to bother them with opening the manually operated door and pulling out the boxes they'd stored around the vehicle.

She should have known Camilla was up to no good. Their first stop had been Target. Cynthia had stocked up on a good deodorant and hand sanitizer while her step-sister had disappeared around the corner.

"Damn, no selection," her stepsister had said, visibly disappointed. "I'd wanted to buy you a going-away gift."

"I'm good," Cynthia had said. "I don't know how I'm going to get this pack closed short of sitting on it and hoping the zippers hold."

"I can't let my favorite stepsister go to Europe without a little something from me."

"I'm your only stepsister," she'd said.

Ten minutes later they'd turned left on a street called Wickeden. "Are you taking me to a wicked den of iniquity?" Cynthia asked. Didn't put it past Camilla. Desmond and Billy had turned out not to be her only escapades.

Camilla didn't say a word, just pulled over to the curb and turned off her ignition. Taking her stepsister's cue,

Cynthia hopped out into the warm air. The maple trees were in full leaf. How had she not noticed that spring had come? Scott had left her in the dead of winter and she'd been cold and dead inside since. The earth had turned and the world had moved on. Maybe it was time to—

"Cynthia, stop moving like a snail!" Camilla was already down and across the street. Cynthia hurried to catch up and followed Camilla past a hair salon, flower shop, and store selling vinyl records. She almost stopped in there. Their parents loved those. But she was leaving tomorrow, so she bypassed the record shop. Instead, she followed her stepsister like a good little duckling falling into line. Cynthia was in the shop before she realized where she was.

Her hands swiftly covered her mouth so as not to release a scream of fright at the aisles of toys. Hazarding a glance above the cash register, Cynthia looked at the name of the store carved in big letters on the wall: Mister Sister Erotica. Well, then.

"Why are we here?" she hissed the question, pulling her stepsister into a corner. A man behind the counter looked up from the magazine he was reading. There was no naked woman or man on the cover. It wasn't a skin mag, but a weekly news magazine. He gave her a half-smile, neither creepy nor off-putting. That was a relief, at least.

"Can I help you, ladies?" he asked laying the periodical on the counter.

Cynthia shook her head and pulled harder at her stepsister. They were in a back corner of the store before she could breathe again. Her face was summer-hot, no doubt flushed from neck to hairline.

"I'm trying to get you a going-away present." Camilla chafed under Cynthia's grip.

"What? What could I possibly use from this place?" she asked, not letting go.

Camilla looked up and down at Cynthia's khaki pants and cardigan. "A lot. But everything you need won't fit in that pack." She turned and scanned the shelves. "Here it is!" she said, brandishing a pink and white box not much different than something from the feminine hygiene section of the drug store. There was a kidney bean shaped cut out on the front. Cynthia snatched the box from her hand.

"Cuddle?" She shook the box. Did a guy come in there? That's the only way she could see getting a cuddle, much less hug from something that small, was if there was a blow up doll in there. "What's this?"

"A G-Spot massager," Camilla said baldly.

The behind the counter guy had materialized in their aisle. He plucked it from Cynthia's hands. Opened the box. A pink and white curved silicone...massager emerged. "The shape is designed to give a woman the utmost in self-pleasure," he said with a straight face. "The best part is it doesn't use batteries. You can charge it with your USB cable."

"I didn't want you to have to run around trying to find batteries in foreign countries," Camilla had piped in.

Which is how Cynthia found herself the not-so-proud owner of the so-called Cuddle G-spot massager.

"I didn't pack that," she blurted to the two TSA officers.

"Ma'am. Are you saying that someone has tampered with your luggage?" the blond asked.

"Did you leave it unattended?" the bearded one inquired.

Fearing an all out ground stop and red alert, Cynthia capitulated. "No, it's mine. It's mine."

She pressed the heart shaped off button. The sounds of beeping metal detectors and conveyer belts filled the vacuum of soundlessness left by the device.

The dark-haired one ran a wand over her backpack. Nary a sound peeped from it. They left Cynthia with her massager, a table full of clothes, and an audience of international travelers. Thanking God she had a long layover, Cynthia carefully re-rolled and re-packed every-thing, including the G-spot massager which she tossed into her purse. If she'd endured this embarrassment, surely she should enjoy her stepsister's gift.

FIVE

CYNTHIA SQUEEZED past the guy in the aisle seat, making her way into the premium economy window seat she'd blown the remainder of her cash on. As soon as the jumbo jet reached cruising altitude, she put on her headphones. Ultimately she'd hefted the big backpack into the overhead bins, but had kept the massager in her purse. In no way did she want a repeat of that security incident on the other side of the Atlantic Ocean.

The curved shape of the massager intrigued her, she had to admit. Was there an actual G-spot? Camilla wasn't the authority on much, but she seemed to have more knowledge about sex than the average person. If Cynthia believed her stepsister, she'd believe that every woman was capable of mind-blowing multiple squirting orgasms. And after more than seven years with Scott, she knew for a fact that wasn't true.

Cynthia started speculating on stuff she'd overheard during drunken sorority parties, but she snapped herself back to reality. If Scott hadn't found it, it probably didn't exist. Although Camilla had said he wasn't a particularly skilled lover. But what did her stepsister know? Camilla hadn't been in the trenches with him like Cynthia had. She shook her head, pushing memories of her ex-fiancé at bay.

She wasn't going to rehash every moment of their sex life now. There was nothing to be gained by that. Instead she plugged in the headphone's cord and tuned into a little French movie dialed up from the adult list. It was called the Adventures of Camille. It was the kind of film Scott would have laughed at if he'd seen her watching in the living room when he'd come home from work or a boys' night out.

Forty minutes in, Cynthia shifted in her seat. She'd forgotten how very open about sex the French were. Every scene was filled with sensuality. Camille's adventures were probably a lot like Camilla's. Reaching under her seat, she pulled the hermetically sealed plastic cover from the blanket and draped the faux gray wool over her entire body. She unbuttoned her pants to relieve herself from the constriction. Almost involuntarily, her hand snaked down inside her panties. Camille and a new conquest undressed on screen.

Just one touch, she promised herself. She glanced over at her flying companion. His eyes were riveted to something that kept exploding again and again, defying the laws of physics. But he didn't seem to care about the authenticity of the carefully crafted spectacle.

Cynthia turned back to her own screen. The woman was undressed from the top down. Her eager young lover was fondling her breasts. His thumbs brushed over her nipples again and again until they were as tight as little raisins. Cynthia nearly groaned aloud, practically feeling the fingers of an eager lover on her own aroused and tender flesh.

Unable to keep her hands still any longer, Cynthia pulled the blanket up to her neck. With trembling fingers she unbuttoned the top button of her blouse, then the others. Her front bra clasp was no barrier and in seconds, her own breasts swung free. With a fake shiver to throw her seatmate off the scent so to speak, the other hand joined the first under the blanket. When the on screen lover suckled the Camille's nipples, she snuck her hand up, licked at her finger tip, then abraded her own with the damp digits. Seconds later after another soul deep kiss, the man's head disappeared under the covers. Was he looking for Camille's G-spot?

Cynthia had to know now . . . .

Reaching down into her purse, she pulled the thick pink wand from its dust bag. Glancing at her seat companion, she confirmed he was engrossed. Not even a shift in her direction. She swiftly hid the massager and worked her pants down around her hips. Slipping it in, Cynthia squirmed in delight. This was one thousand times better than Scott's dick. She cringed with guilt at that thought. He'd been her only lover for more than seven years.

Reclining the seat a little farther back, she watched the movie progress. Camille seemed to leap from one bed to another without guilt or remorse. That woman on screen was all about the pleasure. Cynthia pushed the button on the device, hoping the hum wasn't as loud as it had been during her unfortunate encounter with security.

A squeal escaped before she could muffle it with her blanket-covered hand. Cynthia darted her eyes to the left. Nothing. Thank God for noise cancelling headphones becoming the standard on planes. She pushed the button again. Everything tingled from her nipples to her clit. What in the hell had she been missing?

Half her brain tried to follow along with the gyrating flesh on screen. The other half focused on the seemingly endless combinations of speed and vibration the magic wand—as she'd quickly and fondly come to think of it —offered.

Camille was on her hands and knees, breasts bouncing, getting it from behind. Cynthia squeezed one nipple, then the other. Pressed the button turning the speed higher. She gasped again. Something in the air shifted as her seat mate noticed her for the first time. Sparing him a single glance, she realized she didn't mind him watching.

Camille changed position. She lay prone, biting her lips hard. A hairy man grabbed her hair, breasts, rubbed at her center. At least Cynthia thought that was what he was doing. Much of the action was off screen. Mostly faces and Camille's heaving bosoms filled the small screen. But what she couldn't see, Cynthia's imagination filled in.

More than anything in the world, she wanted a man to want her, do those very things to her. She conjured up an imaginary lover. A cross between the two TSA agents. Sandy-haired, tall, not bare-faced, but not a full beard either—the right amount of stubble.

She imagined full but masculine lips teasing hers, whispering in her ear, nibbling down her chin, suckling at her nipples. Rotating the wand and pushing the button nearly made her come out of her seat. She stuffed a bit of blanket in her mouth to muffle the screams. If she hadn't found her G-spot, she was damn close. Or right there. Cynthia stiffened like an ironing board and came harder than she'd ever come before. Harder than she'd ever come with Scott.

"Ma'am."

She felt a poke in her arm. Returning to earth, or the flying bird thirty-eight thousand feet above it, she looked around wildly.

"Would you like chicken and wild rice or filet and potatoes? What kind of wine?"

Dinner. Airplane food. Cynthia said 'chicken' to get

the flight attendant away. She needed a moment alone. Time to readjust her clothes. Reorient her world.

"You looked like you had fun there," the guy next to her said. His smile was faint.

"Think I found my G-spot," she said matter-of-factly, then accepted the tray of microwaved food.

SIX

CYNTHIA LOOKED out the smudged train window at the passing landscape. Switzerland was . . . pretty. But so were France, and Belgium. She was sure Austria would be no slouch in the beautiful European country lineup.

Thankful the high speed train had Wi-Fi, she pulled out her iPad and flicked open various social media sites. She may not have a man in her life anymore. But friends... she had friends galore.

From the looks of the smiling faces peering back at her from the tablet, everybody was fine. Peppy in Providence. Happy in Hartford. Beautiful in Boston. Pregnant in Portland. Everyone but her was coupled up, procreating, making lives for themselves. All Cynthia had was half her paycheck, a sabbatical that was all too quickly coming to an end, and a Eurail pass.

Alone in her six-seat second class cabin, Cynthia

turned away from the dramatic mountains and wide plains and back to the tablet. Social media was the joke forwarding of the nineties and probably the chain mail of her parents' generation. Despite her distaste for the inroads social media had made into her life, she clicked on the 'What's Your Sex Score Quiz' all her friends were doing. Scrolling down the questions ornamented with wild bar and party photos, she ticked the answer boxes.

No, she didn't drink.

No, she didn't go to parties.

No, she didn't have one-night stands.

She wasn't like Camilla after all.

Like a mind reader, it predicted her sex score: a miserable one. Yup, she'd only slept with her college sweetheart. He'd strung her along until he'd grown up, left town, moved on. Scott had left her behind in Smithfield, Rhode Island, population twenty thousand. But that might as well have been twenty the way everyone and her parents were all up in her business.

No one approved of her emptying her savings for an open-ended ticket to Europe. But with time and youth on her hands, if not now, when? She didn't want to be sixty and compiling her bucket list—too elderly to enjoy travel or ogling cute European boys. Cynthia had passed those travelers in every railway station, cane and walkers in gnarled hands.

It wasn't that she didn't want to grow old, because the

alternative wasn't great, but she wanted to enjoy life now while she was young. Slipping the tablet back into her backpack, she pulled out her mp3 player. Scrolling past music, she looked through the podcasts she'd downloaded before she'd started travel. Neither other people's life stories from the smooth talking public radio announcers nor career advice interested her. She clicked on one that had intrigued and scandalized her in equal measures. A sex advice podcast. She couldn't believe there was such a thing. Finally glad she'd worked up the courage to listen to it, she pressed play.

After plugging the buds in her ears, questions from callers and answers from the so-called love guru came her way. Couples hunting for 'unicorns' for threesomes, toys, and how to prepare for anal left her sweating in the cool car.

Cynthia was glad she was alone so no one could see the heat radiating from her chest, stealing up her face and neck. She went to the old-fashioned train window and pulled it down like on a school bus. She pulled a discarded dining car menu from one of the empty seats and fanned herself vigorously.

"Biglietto? Billet? Ticket?"

Cynthia whipped around, catching her hair in the window's crank. "Oh, I, Oh."

"Let me..." The conductor made no attempt to hide his appreciation of her curves.

European men.

It was taking some time to get used to their lack of subtlety.

His cologne reached her first. The stiff fabric of his navy uniform brushed against her next.

Breath sweet with chocolate whispered against her ear as he gently unwound her hair from the knob.

He stepped back, but no more than a wafer-thin slice of air separated them. Bowing her head, she attempted to search for a name tag, but the red leather strap holding his ticket pouch covered the sun shaped badge. The train jerked and he fell against her. The shiny brass buttons were the perfect distance to fall right against her nipples. Her gasp of surprise only brought the buttons in greater contact with her sensitive flesh.

Jesus fucking Christ she must have been hard up for the mere presence of a living, breathing man to get Cynthia riled up so quickly.

Something rubbed against her down low. She attempted to back up, but the window and wood paneled wall were still behind her.

"Ah, *cherie*, I didn't mean to frighten you," the conductor said.

"You speak French?" It was the stupidest question in the world, but the only clear thought she'd had in the last five minutes.

"*Oui*. My family is from Romandie. But I also speak German, Italian, English. What's your pleasure?"

You inside me ricocheted through her brain. Where in the hell was this coming from? Why did she suddenly wish the thing still poking her in the hip was a hard cock and not what it probably was—a holstered ticket punch.

"English, please. I only speak English," she said. "You asked for my ticket?"

The conductor's right hand smoothed down her face. The smell of wool and cologne made for a heady aphrodisiac. Cynthia didn't want to give him her ticket. She wanted to offer up her needy flesh. "Yes. Where are you going?"

"From B-B-Bern to Bordeaux," she stammered. Then Cynthia did what she always did when she was nervous, gave too much information. "I wanted to taste wines before I left for home."

The conductor had stepped back a centimeter or two. In that space, she reached around him for her handbag and pulled out the Eurail pass and train reservation. He lifted the flap of the navy blue jacket, reaching for the hole punch.

The hard pressure *had* been a leather pouch attached firmly to his belt. She let all the air from her lungs in relief. Her imagination had clearly gone into overdrive. He wasn't attracted to her. The conductor had the European penchant for ignorance of American's personal space. That and great cologne.

He stepped back further and dropped the ticket in a seat.

"Thanks for unwinding my hair," she said, trying not to sound disappointed that this man didn't want to do untoward things to her body.

The conductor turned and opened the door to the little suite Cynthia was occupying all by herself. He looked right, then left, then came back in, carefully pushing the handle into place, closing them back in the compartment together.

"I'm going to be...how do you say it...off duty...in a few minutes. You're the last car I have to check. I have some wine from my last ride to Bordeaux. I'd love to share it with you and unwind more than your hair."

Yes. Say yes. Play it cool.

Cynthia wanted to turn her brain off. Instead of speaking, she nodded.

The conductor's nod was officious, and he was out the door. For a long moment, Cynthia wondered if she'd observed an apparition. Had a sexy European man really offered to share wine with her? One that could say the word wine in at least four different languages.

Damn.

She ruffled through her bag, furious that she'd opted not to bring any more makeup than lip gloss on this trip.

Gathering up her meager supplies, she made her way to the bathroom. First she unwound the pretentious pink scarf she'd been wearing too many days. It was a great look on the Italian and French women she'd encountered, but it wasn't for her. Cynthia did the best she could with a fresh tank top, underwear, perfume and aforementioned gloss.

Looking in the mirror, Cynthia found the result not half-bad. Her hair and lips were shiny, her eyes clear.

When she got back to the compartment, she nearly passed it by because the curtain was drawn. But after the last compartment was the door leading to the next car. Doubling back, she pushed open the door. Without his hat or navy brass-buttoned, double-breasted coat, he was simply mouth-watering.

The top two buttons of his shirt were undone, giving her a peek at a heavily muscled chest. The rolled up sleeves revealed strong forearms. Without the hat, she could see he had sandy hair that framed his green eyes.

Damn.

Cynthia nearly walked back out so the woman who deserved this fantasy could come in and claim what was hers.

"It's you I'm waiting for, *ma belle*," the conductor said. He'd lifted the arms between the seats. It now looked like two plush blue couches facing each other. He held up a set of jingling keys. "The compartment is locked from the outside. I told my colleagues that we weren't to be disturbed. Is that what you would like?"

An out. He was giving her one. She didn't want to take it. Instead she grabbed the keys and tossed them on the empty luggage rack above his head.

"I'd like some of that wine."

Carefully, he pulled out delicately curved glasses and a chilled bottle of white with fancy French script on the label. Expert at life on a moving train, efficiently he poured two glasses. Cynthia accepted what was offered and took a big sip. It was probably a *faux pas* of the highest order, but she needed something to beat back the nerves. Because if the conductor didn't stand up, turn around and walk out of this compartment, she was going to sleep with him.

The conductor watched her intently. One hand held the wine to his lips for a sip now and then. The other smoothed along his leg. She watched his hand move up and down, imagining what it would feel like on her naked skin. Suddenly the tank top and skinny jeans that had seemed so daring moments ago felt like a soggy wet blanket. She moved to open the window again, careful not to catch her hair this time.

"I'm Cynthia," she said, letting the air cool her heated flesh.

He stood, finished his wine, set the glass down on the tiny table bolted to the wall, and moved toward her like a panther stalking prey.

"Y-you didn't say your name." She swallowed. Drank more wine. Swallowed again.

"The only thing you need to know, *mon chaton capricieux,* is that I'm here to pleasure you."

Cynthia thought she'd drop dead, but she laid a hand on her rapidly beating heart. No, not dead.

"More wine, please," she squeezed past her lips.

He reached for the bottle and poured her another full glass, never taking his eyes from her. She tried to sip more elegantly this time.

Then the train jerked to a stop, spilling the wine on her tank top. She didn't dare look down. The top was white, the wine was white, she wasn't wearing a bra. Didn't take a genius to have a good idea what the conductor was looking at. What was making him lick his lips in anticipation.

"Let me," he said, pulling the glass from her hand and tossing it out the window. Faintly, she heard the glass shatter on railroad ties and gravel. But his heat was more overwhelming than sound. Two strong arms pulled her close. He slanted his head, closed his eyes and kissed her.

Ten seconds later, her entire body was on high alert. She was going to melt into the floor. A puddle of what was once Cynthia would be the only thing that remained. When had kissing gotten this hot? She'd kissed before but never like this. Never turned her body into nothing but nerves. Never made her mind numb.

She kissed him back. Explored those full Swiss lips.

Ran a hand through that silky hair, across that strong brow, prominent nose. Eventually she settled into the kiss, laying her hand along the strong column of his neck. He pulled away. In the second he moved to change the angle of his head, she missed him with an ache she didn't believe possible for such a short acquaintance. Before he could come back, she took it upon herself to lift her tank over her head.

The conductor paused for a long moment, simply taking her in. He fitted each of his hands against a breast and kissed her again. His fruit and wine tongue stroked against hers like silk. Slowly he eased her down to the seats. He lifted his head to place one of her legs on the plush blue fabric. He placed a firm hand on the other leg, bent at the knee, planted on the floor and pushed it, leaving her legs wide apart.

He kissed his way from her lips to her neck, lingering in the sensitive hollow there. Cynthia shivered in anticipation. She couldn't say what prompted her, but suddenly shyness felt like a waste of time.

She lifted her own breasts toward him. "Kiss me, lick me, suck me," she begged.

"My pleasure," he hummed against her shoulder. Kissing his way down slowly, Cynthia nearly collapsed with the interminable wait for the pleasure she knew was coming. Then he was there. Plumping one breast with his large hand, he pulled the tip between his lips. Unable to stop herself, she nearly bucked off the seats. He placed the other hand firmly between her belly button and her pubic mound, calming her, stilling her movements.

"There's no hurry. Let it build," he ordered. "Americans are always in such a hurry," he tsked softly before pulling the other nipple into his mouth.

Damn, damn, damn. "Don't stop. God, please don't," she said.

"I won't. There's much time before we're in France," he said. She wanted him to talk. That accent was sexy-as-hell. She wanted him to stop talking because any time he was speaking, his mouth wasn't working magic on her body.

The conductor unbuttoned and unzipped her jeans. With finesse she'd never experienced with Scott, he pulled the pants down and off her legs. Her thong was the only scrap of clothes remaining. Suddenly, she felt very naked and lonely.

"What about you?" she asked. Sitting up, she kissed him long and hard, hoping to give him half the pleasure he'd given her with his mouth. Then she moved to slip one button, then the next through the tiny holes. In small measures his chest was revealed. Cynthia was glad for the glimpse by glimpse view. Any more and her eyes would have rolled back in her head from the shock of it.

The *it* was the perfection of his chest. That navy and red uniform hid the goods well. She smoothed her hands against the flat planes of his chest. The muscle was hard, bunching under her exploring fingers. The smell of musk and spice was stronger here. Leaning down, she nuzzled her nose between his pecs, turning to kiss one flat disk of nipple, then the other.

He nearly jumped. Wired. That's what the podcast sex expert called it when men's nipples were responsive. This man was wired. Slipping her hands down, she found his hard erection straining against his wool pants. Their thickness couldn't hide his arousal.

Cynthia pulled the leather strap from its loops. The belt, laden with a hole puncher and other mysterious gadgets, fell to the train floor with a loud clank. With a single tug of her hand, she urged him to rise just enough for her to yank down his pants and underwear.

She was unable to hide her gasp of surprise. The conductor was long, thick, intact. Cynthia tried to stop the shaking in her hand as she moved to grasp his cock. Following his nod of approval, she tried closing her hands around him, but her fingers couldn't reach her thumb—he was that thick. But what she couldn't do with a tight grip, she wanted to make up for in motion. First, she placed a kiss on the tip, already weeping with moisture, then she moved her hand up and down deliberately. He went from impossibly hard to harder in minutes.

"Stop now. I must taste you," he said, pushing her back down. He wrapped her fingers around the armrest closest to the window. With a jerk, the train started again, having boarded and disembarked passengers or gotten additional cars or something. In moments they moved from a slow crawl from the station to swift moment in between the mountain passes.

The conductor moved aside the scrap between her legs, parted her flesh and laid his tongue against her clit. As if that weren't enough to nearly push her over, the train crossed a set of unsteady tracks causing the vibration of his lips and tongue to be amplified a thousand fold. Unable to stop herself, she cried out, the pleasure of an orgasm coming in waves.

"I'm sorry," she said, loosening her grip on the armrest. "I tried to wait."

"There is no reason to wait, *ma belle*. A beautiful woman is capable of endless pleasure. Let me show you."

Before the conductor started in again on her sensitive flesh, she lifted herself up and grasped his cock–with two hands this time—and took him as far back in her throat as she could. Making strong suction, she pulled at him. Back and forth she bobbed her head as much as she could on his oversized flesh.

The conductor's protest was cut short by his capitulation. A large hand cupped the back of her head and urged her on. She pulled away to lick him. The musk was strong here and nearly made her come again. She squeezed her legs together, trying to keep a second orgasm at bay.

Despite his slitted eyes, he appeared to notice her reticence. "*Arrêtez*. Stop. My fantasy when I first saw you was to bring you to orgasm."

"You've already done that," she said, reaching for his magnificent cock again.

"Twice," he stated. From his red leather pouch, he produced a condom. He bit his lip as he slipped the sheath over his girth. Cynthia nearly offered to do it for him, but didn't think that would help any. She was nervous enough as it was, wondering if that would fit inside her. Scott hadn't been...that big.

The conductor lifted her and turned her toward the window. He placed first her right hand, then her left on the metal band at the top edge of the open glass window. He lifted one leg onto a seat. The other on the seat opposite. Exposed was how Cynthia felt. That didn't last long, when his grunt and groan of pleasure at what he was seeing filled the compartment.

One of his thick fingers probed her readiness first, then a second. Without thinking, she pushed back, seeking fulfillment.

"Ah, you're ready. In a moment," he said, slipping his fingers through her slickness to the front where they swirled around her swollen clitoris. She cried out again, but the sound was lost on the European wind.

The conductor notched himself against her opening.

"Breathe, *cherie*," he said. She took a deep breath, then he impaled her.

Filled.

Filled to the hilt. He moved slowly, then with ass slapping swiftness. Like a coiled spring, the tension built slowly, then pulled so tight she thought she'd die. He pulled at her hips and his cock hit at the same exact spot the little pink toy had. Screams of pleasure filled the train compartment. It took a full minute for Cynthia to realize the sounds were coming from her.

"Oh, God, I'm sorry," she spoke against the wind.

"No need to be sorry," he said, still hard, still moving inside her. He stayed that way, slow entrance and exit until the last quivers left her flesh.

"I can't," he panted. "I have to."

"Come, my conductor, please do."

With a rush of movement, he impaled her again and again. Intertwining her fingers between his, she placed them on her swaying breasts. His grip tightened as he got closer. The train slowed with a jerk, and set the conductor over the edge. "*Mon dieu*," he said, then lost the rhythm, spasming inside her. Cynthia lost her grip on the window and reality as a third orgasm rippled through her.

They collapsed in a heap on the row of chairs.

"You looked so...shy...maybe that's not the word. So saddened when you got on the train, that backpack dwarfing you," the conductor said. "I needed you to know that you're a man's fantasy. Never forget that," he said. "I must go now," he said. "Maybe I'll see you on another trip?"

Cynthia nodded. "Maybe." Though she didn't think she'd survive another encounter with the conductor. He was a maestro. A woman only needed one lesson with a maestro in her life.

SEVEN

THREE MONTHS LATER...

THE TWO HUNDRED passengers had sat on the tarmac a half hour after landing while the airport found a gate for the plane. After sixteen straight hours of travel Cynthia was ready to get the hell off this flying hunk of metal and back into a comfortable bed. The minute the flight attendants opened the doors, she pushed her way forward and into the jet way. She followed the signs, mercifully in English, to baggage claim.

Impatiently Cynthia tapped her foot, waiting for the pack to come around the carousel. The minute it did, she grabbed it and hauled it on her back. Through the sliding doors she went. Camilla was waiting right outside like she'd promised.

"You look different," Camilla said straight off. "Your hair, tanned skin, solid arms. Wow. Europe agreed with you."

"I liked the trains the best," she said. She would never forget the train from Italy to Switzerland.

"Did you miss Scott?"

For long seconds, Cynthia tried to work out who Camilla was talking about. Then it hit her. The fiancé who'd dumped her. It felt like a lifetime ago. "Not for a single second," she said. "You were right. One cock makes you forget the other."

They filled the air with laughter. Cynthia linked arms with her stepsister, glad to be home ready for the adventures that lay ahead.

Camilla

Camilla can't have just one.

On the verge of boredom with her boyfriend Brad, sexually adventurous Camilla gets an invitation to a swinger's club. But when her lover is ravaged by jealousy, Camilla must play her kink card before her relationship comes to an end.

ONE

CAMILLA HORNE CURLED and uncurled her toes. All that toe action wasn't because she was in the throes of ecstasy, but because she was bored out of her mind.

"Brad, it's not working for me right now," she whispered, grabbing at the curly dark hairs on the top of her boyfriend's head. A head that was in between her legs at the moment, going down on her like she was an ice cream sundae.

Blue eyes gazed into hers. Everything about her boyfriend was nearly perfect. From his ocean blue eyes, to his straight aquiline nose, he was the best looking guy she could imagine. Normally when he went down on her with his sexy five o'clock shadow stubble, she came more than once. Not tonight.

When he looked up at her, Brad's mouth was glistening wet, his lips a bright pink. "I love the way you taste, hon. But I love your screaming orgasm even better."

That kind of talk normally turned her on.

Not today.

Falling back against the pillow, Camilla threw an arm over her eyes. Took a deep breath. What was it that was making what should be pleasure, near torture? Wouldn't a thousand women give up their place in line for a ten-thousand-dollar designer bag and take the hot guy instead? A *really* hot guy who loved giving head more than receiving?

She'd dimmed the lights. Not that Camilla was ashamed of her body or anything, but she'd been trying to create a mood. She'd studied *The Joy of Sex* and *The Kama Sutra*. It was all about mood and technique. She had both in spades.

Turning her head left, she saw the reflection of the candlelight flickering on the wall. Whipping her head over to the right, she watched the little LED bars danced up and down on the speaker. Some singer with a low, sultry voice was belting out tunes about sex and grinding and getting it on.

Still nothing.

Brad's hands snaked up and squeezed her tits. His thumbs first grazed her nipples then his fingers joined in, pinching and releasing. All of it, the tongue, his fingers, would normally have her at the edge, then right over. But at this exact moment an orgasm seemed farther away than China.

"Baby, you want me to get Walter?"

"Yeah. Get him," Camilla said. The bed shifted as her boyfriend got up and left the room. Just the mention of Walter made the tips of her breasts harden into little pebbles.

Cool air blew between her legs, but her clit nearly buzzed in anticipation.

A door slammed. "Got him," Brad said.

Oh yeah!

"Walter wants a taste of that sweet little mouth of yours," Brad started.

Hard and warm, Walter slipped in between her lips. She sucked like the fountain of youth was inside him.

"Now he wants to rub along those rock-hard nipples," Brad whispered.

Camilla closed her eyes, reveling in Walter's touch, wet and firm, rubbing first across one nipple then the other.

"Baby, Walter needs that sweet, sweet pussy of yours. It's the only thing that will make up for being left at home all alone all day while you work."

Walter trailed down from her breasts, over her belly, stopping to tickle her navel. In anticipation, Camilla sucked in her stomach.

Oh yeah. One cock was one thing. Two cocks were two hundred percent better.

Then Walter was inside. In and out, he drilled her. This is what she loved about Walter. He was never tired. He was always up for fucking her, even until the sun came up. Even if she came a thousand times.

"Fuck me, Walter," she cried. And he did.

While Walter worked hard, Brad kissed her ear, sucked at first one breast, taking the whole nipple and areola into his mouth. Goddamn. The first breast left Brad's mouth with a sucking/popping sound, then he took the other into his mouth.

"Bite me," Camilla yelled.

Brad obliged. He sank his teeth into her most tender flesh.

Then, when her boyfriend sucked on her clit this time, she nearly hit the ceiling.

"God yes. Walter...Brad. Don't stop. Fuck me. Suck me."

And they did. After that, nothing mattered, not the light, nor the candles, nor the mood music. Just the buzzing between her legs that went from a flicker like the candles on the dresser, to a smoldering flame, to something damn close to a bonfire.

Yes! Yes!

One minute she was blinded by the best orgasm she'd had in weeks. The next minute, Walter was replaced by Brad. By then, she didn't need long and hard. Fast and hard would work just as well.

Craning her head, Camilla watched the show. She loved seeing her own breasts jiggle like a gelatin commercial when a hard dick moved inside her. Looking down a little farther, she was rewarded with the visual of cock in pussy merging with the feeling of arousal tightening her skin everywhere.

Just like that, the night had gone from total loss to total win.

TWO

WALTER LAY on the side of the bed, discarded. Not wanting her vibrator to be stashed away looking rode hard and put up wet, Camilla bounced from the bed and made her way to the bathroom in the hall. Carefully, with warm, soapy water, she washed Walter and laid him on a clean towel to dry.

She predicted that in about five minutes, Brad would be spread-eagle on the bed snoring, while she twiddled her thumbs trying to do anything to sooth the ache that was still throbbing between her legs.

She tiptoed down the hall and snuck a peek through a slit in the bedroom door. Nailed it—so to speak. Sprawled out on the bed, somehow using up nearly all the space of the king-size, even though he wasn't a king-size guy, lay Brad.

Sneaking her robe from the end of the bed, Camilla

wrapped herself in the hot-pink satin. She closed the bedroom door with an audible click. Avoiding the temptation to peek in again to make sure her boyfriend was dead to the world, Camilla escaped down the short hall.

In the turn-of-the-century apartment she'd lived in for the last three years, she shut herself in the second bedroom, which she used as a place to watch TV and work her way up the career ladder. At least that's what she told herself and her family.

Truth was, she was happy enough at her job. By day she worked on the college's alumni relations. By night, she had relations with the alumni. It was one of many secrets she kept to herself. If there was one thing she'd learned in high school, it was that a secret shared was no longer a secret.

Wireless keyboard cold and hard on her hot, soft flesh, Camilla surfed to her favorite "erotica for women" website. Not for the first time, she wondered if there was something wrong with her. Most women she'd met—who would openly discuss sex, and that wasn't the hugest number—wanted to cuddle after they'd done the deed.

The last thing Camilla ever wanted to do in bed was cuddle.

Sex addict.

Insatiable.

Those were two of the nicer names she called herself.

Vowing not to fall into the world of recriminations,

Camilla pressed the spacebar, letting the video play. Fifteen-on-one was one of her favorite themes. This week's girl looked nothing like her, though. Sometimes the girl would have short, mouse-brown hair, and be built like her. Medium in boobs, butt, and stature, most guys walked right by her on the street. Especially if she wasn't strutting her stuff.

When she wanted to catch a guy's attention, she knew how to do it. Hot-pink lipstick was her signature color. She had a chocolate-leather skirt that more than one guy had pushed up her hips in a hurry. Couple that with a sheer top and no bra, and the guys who didn't take a second look at medium-brown Ginny did a double take at Neapolitan Camilla.

She'd tried it for the first time years ago. Most of her college friends had hated frat parties. Camilla had loved them. If she could get away with going to them today, she would. But a woman her age knew better. That's what hookup apps were for. Swiping had saved her from the gritty back pages of the personals. And it had kept her secrets, secret.

Closing her eyes to the acres of flesh on the screen, Camilla probed the recesses of her mind for her favorite memory...

THREE

WITH SOME PRODDING from her friends, a year after graduation, Camilla had sworn off stupid college parties because no graduate needed to be partying like she was seventeen years old. But on the way to her kitchen to get another chocolate sandwich cookie—something her twenty-something figure didn't need—she'd heard the crunch of the lavender flyer under her bunny slipper. She'd taken the paper rather than say no thank you to a cute, hunky guy hanging outside her office. No way was she going to tell him she was no longer an undergrad, but one of the faceless administrative people who actually ran the college.

"The Alpha Ro Progressive" stared back at her in hastily scrawled and photocopied script. Forgetting her sweet tooth for a moment, she'd bent and picked up the paper.

It promised that each member of the fraternity would have an all-original drink in their room. A good drink or two to escape the doldrums of life after college had been exactly what Camilla needed.

Twenty minutes later, she was dressed in a sparkly mini skirt, tight tank, and heels too tall for doing more than teetering around. Thirty minutes later, she was getting her hand stamped by the cuties on door duty. While a lot of underage kids on campus resented the college's policy of fraternities checking IDs at the door, Camilla had always looked at it as another opportunity to meet a new guy.

Tonight's check proved to be no exception. The two guys each bussed her on the cheek and welcomed her in the door.

Now, this—this was her kind of party.

"Where'd you get the drink?" she asked a girl who whipped past with a blue plastic cup in her hand.

Camilla followed the girl's index finger toward an open bedroom door. All four walls were decorated in white and green.

"You a Michigan State fan?" Camilla asked.

The guy stirring a red concoction in a bowl nodded. "Ready for the Eight Mile?"

"What's that?"

The boy ladled a generous portion in a red plastic cup. "All the girls love it. Try it."

Accepting the drink, Camilla took a generous sip. It

was the best-tasting thing she'd had in days, and it was going straight to her head. "What the hell?"

"Rum, whisky, and brandy—"

"Stop there," she said, kissing her cup with his. "Cheers."

The next room—well, suite—had another red drink. "What's this one?"

"El Presidente," the guy said. Camilla cocked her head awkwardly. She hoped it wasn't hanging off her neck by a mere thread, because it sure felt that way. The rum, whisky, brandy combo had gone straight to her head. Maybe dinner should have been more than a couple of cookies.

"Are you the president?" she asked, setting down the cup on a small table right by the door. This guy was cute and she wanted to be sober enough to groove on his assets. They were all too easy to appreciate in his tight tank and nylon running shorts. She couldn't keep herself from staring. Either he was stuffing some kind of tube sock down his shorts, or the guy was packing...something.

"Billy Moran, at your service," he said with a flourish of his arms. His dark hair was spiked straight from his scalp. His eyes crinkled at the corners. His smile was infectious. She smiled back, admiring the little dimple in his chin. She scanned his body.

Those arms. Biceps as thick and strong as tree

branches reached out, lifting her with no effort, and moved her from the door.

Camilla was glad of Billy's split-second timing because a troop of guys and girls spilled through the entrance a second later. Another sex-on-a-stick guy picked up a remote. Music blared though invisible speakers, a thumping bass beat nearly shook the pennants off the walls.

She downed the rest of the second red drink. An anonymous hand removed it from hers. Appropriately liquored up, she started to dance with the beat. Soon a couple of the other girls joined in, then the boys.

One song bled into another. The room got hotter, and Billy and another boy helped her remove her too-hot sequined top, leaving her in nothing more than a camisole that left little to the imagination. But she didn't want them to imagine, she wanted them to see.

Billy moved behind her, holding her hips between his large hands and moving with her to the music. If the ridge riding her butt was any indication, Billy didn't want to leave much to the imagination either.

"I'm Desmond," another guy said, his hands landed on her ribs, right below her breasts. For two or three songs, it continued that way, one hot guy—in every sense of the word—in the front. The other in the back. Every couple of minutes, she lifted her arms, executing a twirl. Both guys were as hard as rocks.

"Wanna come to my room?" Desmond asked, his breath a whisper in her ear.

"Saw her first," Billy said loudly enough for all three of them to hear.

"Boys, boys," Camilla chided, full of laughter. For a moment a thought seared her brain. Why in good name couldn't she have both at the same time? Now *that* would be fun.

The suggestion almost left her lips, but her courage flagged at the last moment. Hooking her fingers in Desmond's belt loop, she made her choice then let him lead her to a very quiet room on the other side of the sprawling Georgian mansion.

FOUR

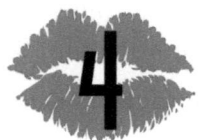

ONCE HE CLOSED the heavy wood door, the only sound other than their breathing, was the faint thump of heavy bass.

Camilla leaned against the closed door, taking in the room around her. Clothes, books, and guy stuff littered the small space. Then she took in Desmond. He was model perfect, green-eyed, and square-jawed. His jet black hair was cut close to his scalp framing his perfect face. She'd seen him around campus, and his bedroom skills were legendary.

"We have plaster walls," Desmond said. He lifted his arms and placed them on the door, framing her. His lips were full and masculine, a distraction from what he was saying.

"Plaster?" Her rum-soaked brain could make little sense of building materials.

"It makes a good sound barrier. I work construction in the summer," he explained.

She wrapped as much of her hand as she could around his biceps. "It suits you."

"That's not why I told you that," Desmond said, his voice hoarse. His breathing was getting heavier by the moment. "I'm telling you this, because when I make you come, I want you to know you can scream without anyone hearing you."

"How do you know I'm a screamer?" Camilla asked, trying for coy.

Desmond licked first her top lip, then her bottom. "Maybe not a screamer. Doesn't matter how you show it. I'm gonna make you come hard before you even get a piece of this," he finished. He pulled one of her hands from his arm and molded it to the front of his button-fly jeans.

"This is what I'm here for," she whispered then closed her hand around as much of him as she could with stiff denim separating flesh from flesh.

"Whoa. Slow down, sister," he said. "Lift your arms all the way up."

She did as she was told. In one swift motion, Desmond liberated her of the camisole top she'd painstakingly chosen only a couple of hours earlier. She didn't miss the scrap of fabric one bit, though. The look of hunger on his face was enough to make her forget all about clothing.

For a single moment, Camilla hesitated. It was one

thing to contemplate a one-night stand while looking in your closet for the right outfit. It was another to be on the verge of sex with a stranger. Rebound sex at that.

"You okay?" Desmond asked. His voice had gone from come hither to concern.

Shit. That was not the vibe she'd set out to create. But her ex, Tony, dumping her like a sack of rotten fruit, had taken its toll.

"I'm perfectly fine," Camilla said, hoping she'd feel perfectly fine if she kept repeating that line in her head.

"You are *fine*, that's for sure," Desmond said. The normally cheesy line was delivered with such sincerity that Camilla felt a whole lot better.

"Do you keep your promises?"

"Always. I like the way the skirt looked on your ass while dancing. You don't need that anymore," he said. Desmond's hands rested at her waist. But when she expected a frantic shove of her clothes, she got a kiss instead. The meeting of lips was a surprise.

It didn't fit into her definition of a one-night stand. It was nice though. Really nice. When his mouth opened and their tongues met, it got a whole lot hotter in the room. Breaking the kiss, Camilla shoved down her own skirt. If he kissed that good...

Sensing her impatience, he pulled them back to the bed. Anticipation made the short walk to the bed unsteady.

He threw off the comforter, exposing blue plaid flannel sheet.

"Lay on your stomach," he ordered.

She wasn't even tipsy anymore, but the thought of this boy putting his hands on her, had her feeling as high as she'd felt minutes after she'd downed those first drinks.

She'd worn no bra under her camisole and her nipples made immediate contact with the rough cotton. Camilla wanted to wallow in that sensation, but Desmond was skimming her lace thong down her legs and the cool night air from the open window blowing on her most private areas barely cooled the heat pooling at her core.

Warm hands and cool liquid hit her backside all at once.

"What—"

"Shhh. I'm keeping my promise," he said.

The liquid went from cold to warm in moments as Desmond's hands glided up and down her body. First, he kneaded her shoulders and neck, instantly relieving any tension.

Warm hands slipped down to the small of her back. Up again, they skimmed along the sides of her tits. Fingers brushed against her nipples. Biting her lip kept in her gasp of surprise at the level of arousal he'd built in such a short time.

Up and down they went. Then they spun over her

bum, one time, a second time... She nearly jumped from the bed when his seeking fingers brushed against her sex.

"Fuck!"

"With my fingers, then," he said. Then a thumb slipped into her. It wasn't a cock, but Desmond bent his thumb in such a way that it jolted her clit to life. He didn't let his remaining fingers go to waste. They parted her flesh and each one brushed against her bud. Each flutter no harder than the one before.

"Hard. I need it hard," Camilla cried.

Desmond didn't hesitate. The fingers pressed hard, rubbing first side to side, then up and down. He plunged the thumb into her once, twice. The third time it pushed her over the edge.

"Oh, yeah!" she heard Desmond shout in triumph. "I love a screamer."

FIVE

SHE MELTED INTO THE BED. Cologne and sex mingled in the air. "That was—"

"Number one."

"You weren't kidding?"

"I don't kid about coming," he said. "Turn over."

Willingly, Camilla rolled over. Desmond straddled her.

"Take off your clothes," she begged.

He whipped his shirt over his head. Camilla slipped a single finger behind his belt loop. "The rest?"

"Not yet," he said. His hands slipped right to her tits. He squeezed, plumped, then rubbed his palms over her nipples. They went from semi-hard to painfully tight in seconds.

"Don't stop," she pleaded. Previous lovers had called

her voracious. This was the first time she'd ever met someone who could meet her appetite.

He didn't stop. His hands left her breasts and smoothed down her body until they came to her thighs. Gently, he separated her folds. Cool air was replaced by a whoosh of warm breath. She could feel her clit swell under his scrutiny. He studied her like he was making a plan of attack. Before she could squirm in embarrassment at his frank admiration, he mouth replaced his eyes. Relentlessly, he painted her with his tongue. Five seconds or five minutes later, explosions made stars appeared behind her eyelids.

"Your turn," Camilla said when she was able to catch her breath. Desmond was now standing at the foot of the bed, his hand gripped tight on the fabric that was undoubtedly chafing against his dick.

Sitting up, her legs straddling his, she didn't take no for an answer this time. Her hands went straight to his belt. She pulled the leather apart, unsnapped the jeans at the waist, then unbuttoned the fly as quickly as she could manage. The pants and buckle clanged against the scarred wood floor. He kicked them off with a single motion. Rising to her knees, Camilla pushed her way past his waistband and pulled his cock from the too-tight underwear that had been holding it in place.

Damn.

It was the longest dick she'd ever seen. She couldn't imagine how she'd fit all of him inside her.

Kicking that can down the road, Camilla lowered onto her back.

"My turn," she said. In one hand, she held his cock firm, a little up and down swirling motion keeping him as hard as a steel rod. Opening wide, she took one of his balls in her mouth, then the other.

"Enough," he said. She released him and he stalked to a desk on the far side of the room. When he came back, a purple-and-blue condom sheathed his cock.

"Are those the frat's colors?"

"You know it," he said, spinning her and pulling her butt to the edge of the mattress. "You're about to get Alpha Rode," he said before impaling her with his magnificent length.

"More...harder..."

"At your service," he said before pulling out and slamming into her hard. The wind-up started again. Every touch, every sensation was amplified by what had come before. Missionary wasn't always her favorite, but it worked for her now. Gripping his biceps hard, she held on for dear life. When he slowed for a moment, she let go of his arms and smoothed her hands across the wide expanse of his chest. He was hard everywhere. Before she could explore, Desmond had flipped her over again.

"Hands and knees," he said.

She obeyed. For a long moment nothing happened. Then one hand squeezed one pendulous breast, while the other delved into the cream between her folds before smearing it everywhere. When his fingers brushed against her clit, she nearly collapsed.

Unable to keep the moans quiet or soft, Camilla let loose everything she was feeling, desired, fulfilled, satisfied. It was so fucking great, it was almost too good to be true —almost.

A few seconds later, he withdrew.

"I want to be on top," Camilla said.

"Just what I had in mind," he responded, lying back on the mussed bed.

She climbed up on him and eased herself down slowly. "Oh, my god," she groaned. He filled her completely. Leaning forward, she grabbed at the hard caps of muscle on his shoulders. Carefully, she moved up and down, taking all of him slowly but surely.

"Damn, you're so big."

"It's so fucking hot that you can fit all of me," he said, grabbing at her tits. He pulled her forward, sucking one nipple hard, then the other.

Camilla ramped up her speed. Up and down, she sank on his dick time and again, until his hands and mouth stopped squeezing, licking, and biting. She fucked him until he was a pool of groans and shouts.

Desmond grabbed her hips, holding her still as he

pumped powerfully once, twice, and a third time. One shout and he was still.

She climbed off and collapsed in a heap next to him.

"Damn, girl," he said before heaving himself up and walking through a small door in the corner of the room. She heard a flush, and Desmond was back.

Camilla waited for sleep to claim him, like it did all men. When his chest rose and fell, she found her clothes and put them back on.

SIX

THE PARTY MUST HAVE MOVED SOMEWHERE ELSE because the hallway was quiet. Camilla looked left and right, trying to remember the way out.

"Pssst."

She swiveled around, trying to locate the hissing sound.

"Pssst."

Camilla craned her neck.

"C'mere," she heard.

"Billy?"

He hefted a blue plastic cup. "Electric lemonade."

She walked around the corner toward the outstretched hand.

"Electric?"

"Aw, it was the best I could come up with on short notice," he said.

She looked more closely into the alcove at the end of the hall. There were two doors. The first was obviously Billy's huge room, where he'd served the flame-red drink. The other was some kind of tiny closet with a tiny sink and urinal. The urinal was filled with something bright yellow.

"Wait..."

"We don't use it. I thought it would be funny if the lemonade came from a urinal."

"Did anyone laugh?"

"Not exactly," Billy said.

Camilla took a sip. The lemon taste was spiked heavily with vodka and something else.

"What else is in here?"

"Silver tequila."

"Cool," she said. It *was* cool, and sweet, and a whole lot of good.

Billy leaned against the doorjamb, but his casual pose didn't hide nervousness. She wondered if she made him tense. It was kind of weird because he didn't seem tense at all on the dance floor.

"What's up?"

Billy pulled her inside the room. He leaned down and whispered in her ear, though there was no one around. "I like a buttered bun."

A thrill snaked up her spine. Half of her brain was filling with hope that he meant what she thought he meant. The other half was nearly sure that couldn't be the case. It would be too weird for him to want the same thing as her. Except for Desmond, she'd never met anyone who'd even wanted to try keeping up with her.

She walked farther into the room. Setting her drink down on the dresser, she looked at Billy from under her lids.

"Do you mean hot cross buns, dinner rolls, or me?"

"I could hear you from down the hall. Gave me a raging boner."

Slinky like a cat, Camilla moved toward Billy. His loose shorts gave her the access she needed. With a single hand, she pushed the bedroom door closed. With the other, she shoved him against the hard wood. As she kept him pinned, the index and middle finger of her other hand walked up his thigh. Nearly all of the breath left him in a whoosh.

One step with her fingers, then two, then ten got her where she wanted to be. Under all the nylon, he was as hard as a rock. Where Desmond had been impossibly long, Billy was massively thick.

Camilla turned to scope out the room. Billy's bed was covered with books. Well, that wasn't going to work. Looking around, she spied a huge cowhide on the floor. Kicking off her heels, she tested it with her toes. It was softer than she'd thought it would be.

For the second time that night, she shimmied out of her

clothes. Kicking them to the side, she knelt, then sat, and ultimately lay on her side.

"Jesus—"

"Isn't here, Billy Moran, but I am."

"It's like a fucking fantasy come true. If I touch you, will you disappear?"

"Come, yes. Disappear, no. Take off your clothes."

Billy stopped moving like he was in quicksand. His movements sped up and the Alpha Ro t-shirt and shorts disappeared in a moment. Yet, he stood still.

Not *exactly* still. His cock twitched with every heartbeat pushing blood down, making him harder and thicker.

He walked to the edge of the rug. It took a lot for him to kneel down and not injure the goods.

"Come closer. It won't break."

"It feels pretty damn close to it."

"I think I can help you with that," she said. Reaching out, she wrapped her hand around his cock. She was surprised that her thumb couldn't meet her fingers. That, she hadn't expected. Camilla thought she'd seen it all.

"Some girls—"

"Some girls aren't me. I love cock in every shape and form. And this, sir, is a most excellent shape."

Camilla lowered her head and swirled a tongue around the engorged head. After she pulled her lips away with an audible pop, his cock went from crimson to purple.

Oh, this was going to be good.

Opening her jaw, Camilla took him as deep as possible, getting him good and wet. As wet as she was.

"Damn, girl. I...I...can't do this."

"I want you to fuck me, Billy."

Lying back, Camilla let her knees fall open. Inch by inch, she smoothed her hand down her neck, across her tits, and skimmed her stomach. Splaying her fingers, she nudged herself open to Billy's gaze with her index and ring fingers. The middle finger slipped over her clit, arrowing exactly where she wanted him.

Billy hesitated only a second more. He pulled on a striped condom. Taking his cock in his fist, he notched it at her opening.

"God, you're tight."

"Damn, you're big."

But she wanted this—so much. Taking a deep breath, she relaxed her muscles as much as she could. Centimeter by centimeter, he stretched and filled her. She sucked in a breath as he went all the way. Unable to hold back, she let out a keening cry of pleasure with her exhale.

"Oh, fuck. Make some noise, girl. I love the sounds you make. You're so hot and wet," Billy said between puffs of air. He grabbed her thighs and laid her heels on his shoulders. With a firm grip on her legs, he sped up the pace.

Camilla couldn't have kept quiet if she'd wanted to.

Movement from the corner of her eye caught her attention.

Billy's door was open a crack and the faces of two or three other frat brothers poked around the side, their pale faces standing out in contrast to the dark wood.

If the guys of Alpha Ro wanted a performance, she was going to give it to them.

Placing a perfectly manicured nail between her teeth, Camilla made sure her finger was good and wet. Rubbing it over one nipple, then the second, made Billy pump even harder and faster.

One of the Alpha Ro guys looked like he was going to pop a vein. She let the finger travel across her belly, only to disappear between her folds. Locking eyes with each of the boys at the door in turn, Camilla let go of all inhibitions. Every "Fuck me", "Oh god", and "Oh Yes" was heartfelt. She wanted Billy to come hard, and leave his brothers with something to stroke to a little later.

Billy broke his rhythm for a second.

"You close?" she asked.

The eyes that had been closed in concentration opened. Sky blue eyes met hers. "So. Damn. Close."

This night had been all about taking risks. So she took a shot that his fantasies were a lot like to hers.

"Did you like hearing Desmond do me? There's a line out the door of guys ready to do me too. When you come, I'll be ready for your frat brothers."

As much as she could around his thickness, Camilla squeezed.

Billy's hoarse shout let her know she was successful. She continued milking him dry.

SEVEN

"WHAT ARE YOU DOING, CAMILLA?"

Hearing Brad's voice was like seeing a ghost. Billy, and Desmond, and Alpha Ro disappeared from her mind like smoke.

In her panic, Camilla couldn't think what to do first, so she tried to do it all at the same time—straighten her clothes, press the off button on the monitor, and close the web page.

The keyboard in her lap clattered to the floor.

"Checking e-mail," she said in response. The false answer stuttered out like the lie it was. Camilla continued pressing buttons, hiding the evidence of her betrayal.

"A lot of naked guys sending you mail?" Brad arched an eyebrow. But his sharp tone did nothing to mask the hurt feelings he was shitty at covering up.

"No, Brad. No naked men send me mail. I'm a one-man woman."

"Not if you count Walter," he said.

With everything covered up, she swiveled around in the chair. With a critical eye, she surveyed her long-time boyfriend. He was fine. More than that, he was *fine*.

Blue eyes rimmed with gray searched her face. His longish hair was perfect for grabbing when they were kissing, when they were face-to-face, when he was eating her out. He ran almost every day, so his six-pack had stayed firm while his friends had gone soft with their beginning beer guts.

He was *fuckable*. There was no doubt about that. On top of all that, he was dedicated to her. He wasn't a user like Tony, the guy she'd cooked and cleaned for, only to be dumped when a better-looking girl came along.

Camilla looked at the ring she wore on her index finger. She'd bought it after the night at Alpha Ro. The three roses stood for the most men she'd slept with in a single night.

Brad would never go for that. Walter had been enough of a hard sell.

"Are you jealous of a vibrator?"

"I'm not fucking jealous of a piece of vibrating silicone."

"Sure sounds like it. I *like* Walter. He adds a little—"

"A little what, Camilla?"

"Girls can have multiple orgasms—"

"I get you off at least twice, when you let me."

Such fragile egos men had. "They say the third time is a charm, right?"

"You didn't seem that interested until Walter came out," Brad said. "You kind of haven't been all that interested *unless* Walter comes out."

Which was a thousand percent true. Things had been good with Brad. Almost verging on great. He got her jokes. They biked together, cooked together, and until a few months ago, the sex had been great.

Then she'd discovered sexychatpad.com and the fetish community. She'd only been exploring out of boredom on a night not unlike this one. Brad had come and gone to sleep, and she'd been left horny and wide awake.

She'd created a free e-mail address and signed up. Not three days later, she found an invitation in her inbox. Three insatiable ladies were needed for a gangbang.

Camilla had signed out as fast as she could. It had been like giving that first hit to a potential addict. Something had told her if she clicked, she wouldn't ever be able to go back to vanilla sex and Brad.

"Is it someone else?" Brad asked, interrupting her straying thoughts.

"Uh...um...no."

"Oh my god, you've met another guy."

"No. Brad. No, I haven't met anyone else I want to be with."

"Why did you hesitate?"

"Because I don't know what to say. I don't know what's wrong exactly."

"Our relationship is solid, Camilla. Why are you trying to sabotage it? I never thought you were *that* girl, looking for bad boys and drama."

"I'm not that girl. Look, I like sex...a lot. Maybe we have mismatched libidos."

"So now you're saying I can't satisfy you."

Damn. Fragile ego injured. She laid a conciliatory hand on his arm. This conversation was quickly spiraling out of control. "You satisfy me just fine."

"Didn't seem that way a half hour ago."

"I came. I love you. I love what you did with Walter. Sometimes I just need a bit more."

"Like now?" Brad's eyes had gone a bit hazy. He was ready for an unprecedented second round. Usually he was a one-and-done guy. Once he was asleep, she was on her own.

"Very much now," Camilla said, lowering her voice to husky range. "Very much."

For once, Brad didn't light the candles, pull back the covers, and talk about every move before he made it.

Instead he shoved up her nightgown, pulled off her boy shorts. Her boyfriend's face was intense. His hands cupped her shoulders and walked her back to the windowsill. She slipped her bare butt on the cold wood... It was a kind of exquisite pleasure/pain that ignited a cold fire.

Without preamble, Brad shoved down his boxers. He was as hard as a steel rod. Before she could inhale, he'd pressed himself home. Fast and hard, he took her. She didn't have a chance to breathe or grab on for dear life. One second she was worried about falling. The next second she was falling in a good way.

The orgasm that hit her was the best that night. For long seconds she wasn't thinking about Billy, Desmond, Walter, or a train of guys. For that moment, Brad was enough.

EIGHT

FOR TWO WEEKS, Camilla wished, prayed, and hoped Brad would always be enough for her. But sexychatpad.com was like a gateway drug. One or two orgasms with Brad and Walter weren't enough.

But Camilla had taken the bait the internet dangled before her and had signed up for a kink website and a swingers' club. Even in little old Providence, there were way more people out looking for multiple partners than she ever thought possible.

After days of poking around the sites long after Brad had gone to sleep, she'd finally worked up the nerve to hit the contact button. Work was a safe cover, so she brought her tablet to her office. While she had no intention of joining one of these parties, she wanted to do more investigation while she was awake, alert, and safe from prying eyes.

During her lunch hour, she skipped the salad and got down to business. The kink site listed masters who could arrange gangbang sessions at local hotels. The swingers' site had a whole house dedicated to debauchery.

Discreetly tucked away in a turn-of-the-last-century Victorian, some of Rhode Island's more sexually adventurous had set up a club.

She lifted her finger from the tablet screen. With a single click, she could be granted her greatest wish.

She wanted to tap on one of the buttons so much, it was hell keeping her finger from the screen. Instead, she tapped the message icon and asked for help from the one person who wouldn't judge her—too much.

"YOU'RE DRINKING SELTZER?" Cynthia asked several hours later while nursing her own Cosmo at the swanky new happy hour in a revitalized downtown jewelry factory.

Camilla tried not to roll her eyes. She'd work on getting her step-sister to try something different one of these days.

"I need to be sober." Camilla was never one hundred percent sober at a bar.

"Uh-oh, is this about Brad?"

She sipped her mineral water, wishing for something stronger. But she'd spent nearly a decade making decisions about her sex life under the influence of alcohol. For once she wanted to make a sober, mature, thought-out decision. Isn't that what adulthood was all about?

"It's not really about Brad, but about me," sober Camilla revealed.

"Ooooookay."

"How many guys have you been with?" Camilla asked baldly.

Cynthia hesitated a long minute. "Three. But you already know this."

"Do you ever wish you had more partners?"

"I'm single and looking..."

"No. I mean do you wish you'd had more experience? It took plane tickets to Europe and a rail pass for you to do the one-night-stand thing."

Cynthia blushed furiously. "I've never been like you. I lost count in high school of the guys you'd done."

"I'm sorry to put you on the spot like this. I'm deflecting. Here's the thing. I'm thinking of breaking up with Brad."

"Because you're bored, right? Some other guy has caught your eye. You'll never get married if you're always chasing the next dick."

Ah, god. The marriage and family propaganda had begun.

"I don't want to get married, first of all. Chasing dick is fun, second of all."

"Third of all? What's wrong with Brad?" Cynthia

asked, looking genuinely perplexed. In her step-sister's mind, she and Brad had probably already walked down the aisle, bought a house in Barrington, and filled it with two-point-three kids.

"He doesn't turn me on."

"But..." Cynthia's voice lowered to a whisper. Camilla could barely hear her above the din of the noisy College Hill patrons. "I thought you guys did it about a million times a week?"

"Well...okay. We're still doing it nearly every day...but it's not the same."

"They say that things change and mature in long-term relationships."

"Who are these sexually bored 'they?'"

"You're bored? Who's to say you won't get bored with the next guy?" Her step-sister was full of common sense. It was why she'd dialed Cynthia's number first. But for all her logic, Camilla still hesitated.

"Well..."

"Goddammit, you have a plan. That was all preamble. What do you want my approval for?"

"Not your approval, exactly. I want to float an idea by you."

"Waiting..."

"Uncross your arms. Un-purse your lips. I want you to be open to the possibilities."

Cynthia relaxed her posture then downed the rest of

her drink in a single gulp. She waived to the bartender. Camilla didn't speak until her step-sister had finished her second drink, and said, "Okay, I'm open now. Hit me."

"I want to do a gangbang."

Camilla was glad that Cynthia's cocktail glass was empty because her step-sister knocked it clear to next week. They watched in silence as the patrons' clapping ceased and a busboy swept up the broken shards of glass.

"Are you serious? No, wait. Have you lost your mind? You're not some porn star. Is that where you got the idea? I told you years ago that you watch too much porn."

"I don't know where I got the idea. But now that it's in my head, I can't shake it."

"And what does Brad think?"

"He doesn't know. But he's kind of figured out I'm bored. He's tried to step up his game. He's even gotten on board with Walter."

"Walter? You've done a threesome?"

"Threesome, yes. Walter is not a he, but an it. He's my vibrator."

"TMI. I still haven't forgiven you for popping that toy in my luggage. I have PTSD from that TSA search."

Camilla took a deep breath. She covered her mouth. She turned away from Cynthia, but nothing could stop the laughter from sputtering up through her lips.

"I'm really sorry. Okay, only kind of sorry. It got you loose enough to do the stranger-sex thing."

"One guy. A single one-night stand. You're talking about, what, a dozen guys?"

"The two groups I've found say it's usually five to ten guys depending."

"Groups? This isn't idle speculation, is it?"

"I've found a couple of people who organize such things."

"In Providence?"

"It's way kinkier than you'd think."

"So we're back to you cheating on Brad."

"I don't want to break up with him. Except for him having only one dick, he's a great guy."

"Do you think you could do it once and get it out of your system?"

"You mean not tell him?" That was out there for conventional Cynthia.

"I'm thinking out loud here. I don't know. Maybe it's something you *could* get out of your system. Like the Bolder Dash."

"I did bug your dad a bit," Camilla admitted.

"We'd only done the *Brady Bunch* thing with your mom marrying my dad, and you were nagging Dad about driving to Bristol."

"What does a roller coaster have to do with sex?" I asked. I didn't want to rehash one of my earliest memories of us all as a blended family.

"You cried when Dad got you Lake Compounce passes

for your birthday. That was the first time we really talked. When you were trying to figure out how to get out of going back to the park."

"The coaster was a disappointment. Didn't want to face that again," I said. Her dad had been really nice. After the first time he'd given in to my begging and taken us all to the amusement park, I'd ridden the big wooden roller coaster that had been relentlessly advertised on TV. To say the ride was anticlimactic would be an understatement. When Cynthia's dad had presented the expensive season passes to me after cake, what could I say? I hated the amusement park, it hadn't lived up to my expectations, I couldn't go back. Ugh. I'd spent a year drinking overpriced soda and eating hot dogs in the sun pretending to be grateful.

"Don't you think this could happen with sex?" Cynthia continued "What if all the guys are hairy and smelly? What if you get some gross STD? What if it does nothing for you?"

"All these years later, I'm glad I did the coaster. Saved me from wasting my time on coasters. Maybe if I do this, the fantasy won't live up to reality. Then I'll know. I'll be able to have a normal, vanilla sex life with Brad."

"You sound like you've talked yourself into it."

"I kinda have."

"So are you going to sell Brad?"

"Who says I have to sell him anything if it's one and done?" Camilla asked, already plotting her next move.

NINE

"WE BOOKED a suite at the hotel near the airport," Erika said over the phone.

Camilla dutifully copied down the room number and directions to Warwick. She'd gone ahead and done it. Arranged for a real sexual adventure.

"Where are you off to?" Brad asked when he walked into the kitchen.

Camilla halfway wanted to tell him. Having him there would make this experience far more comfortable, and even more fun.

He opened the fridge to pull out a beer. Not a can of beer, mind you, but some kind of IPA or ESB or another creation of the alphabet soup that came from the craft breweries popping up in the area.

Sex in her office had been the most out there thing he'd done since Walter. And Walter had been introduced very carefully. This was not a bomb she could drop between happy hour and dinner. She examined her boyfriend closely. Pinstriped boxers and a matching undershirt did not scream monogamish.

"There's a pop-up comedy club tonight at a club near the airport."

"I'd be up for that," he said setting his full beer on the counter. He never drank and drove. Not even a sip or two.

"Girls' night out," she said, gesturing to the beer. "Relax. Enjoy." She took herself to the bedroom and jumped into the shower.

AT EIGHT THIRTY on the cot, she knocked on the door of room 627.

"I'm Erika. And you're Camilla?"

After she nodded at the middle-aged woman, she stared into the hotel room. It looked like about a million others in the world. An all-beige interior and two double beds filled the space.

Finally, she looked back at Erika and extended her hand.

"Camilla Horne."

"Have you done this before?" Erika asked without censure.

"No, but it's something I've wanted to do for a long time."

"Let me give you the rundown. There will be two girls. You and Angel. Ten guys have texted me to let me know they're downstairs. Once Angel gets here and you guys give the okay, I'll give them the room number."

Erika gestured to a desk in the corner. "There's a bucket of wine coolers over there. Some people drink a little to warm up, then we get ready to go. You girls get comfortable, and tell the guys what you want."

There was no music. The whole thing seemed a little antiseptic to Camilla. But life wasn't like the movies, right? Someone had once called porn Kabuki sex. Real life couldn't possibly measure up to an on-screen performance.

The high she'd been experiencing on the drive out came crashing down.

Later, she'd wonder if Erika was psychic. "You want to watch tonight?"

"I don't have to—?"

"Of course not. I should have suggested it earlier. Angel is a pro at this. She loves it. Take that barstool in the corner—"

Whatever else Erika was going to say was lost when a knock came at the door.

Camilla tried hard not to let her insecurities get the best of her, but Angel was va, va, and the voom. Busty, blonde, and attractive. Camilla was suddenly a thousand percent glad, she was only watching. Laying in the second bed waiting to get picked would have been humiliating.

Erika made the introductions. "Angel, Camilla. Camilla, Angel."

"You're new on the scene," Angel said.

Camilla only nodded. Swinger small talk wasn't something she'd mastered.

"She's watching tonight," Erika announced.

"Did you bring your boyfriend? I've never met a man who would turn down a free show."

"He's not into any of this," Camilla said.

"Wow. That's too bad. My boyfriend loves this shit. He'll be one of the guys coming up. So yours is home while you get to have all the fun, huh? I bet you guys will get it on when you tell him what happened tonight, right?"

"He doesn't know I'm here," Camilla blurted out.

Then she closed her eyes against the silence from the two women. Their judgment was practically a tangible thing that hung in the air.

"Oh, honey," Angel said, coming over to Camilla. "You're young. But you'll learn that you have to let your freak flag fly."

"Freak flag?"

"Here, let me lay it out for you—"

She glanced at her watch. "Don't we have to let the guys up?"

"Shit no. I'm gonna make their fantasy come true. They can wait a goddamn second. Here's my little speech. Erika's heard it before, I'm sure."

"Sorting condoms over here," Erika called from the other side of the room.

"When we meet a guy, the first thing we think about is compatibility, right?"

Camilla nodded. So far, so good.

"Do they like the same music, food, TV shows. If you like hard rock, it would be hell living with a country music lover, and vice versa."

"But what does that have to do—"

Angel waved away Camilla's question. "So what do you have in common with your guy?"

"Brad? Well, we both like rap—"

Angel winced. "To each his own."

"We both like the kinds of restaurants that serve beer and nachos. We like action movies—"

"How often do you go to the movies?"

Camilla shrugged. "I don't know. Maybe twice a month?"

"Restaurants?"

"Maybe once a week. Sometimes not even that. Neither one of us much likes to drive in the snow. More in the summer. We both like lobster rolls."

"So you've told me shit you guys do maybe once or twice a month."

"Okay—"

"How often do you guys do the nasty?"

"'Nasty' isn't a word we like to use, Angel," Erika

interjected.

Heat crept up Camilla's neck at the frank talk the women shared. "Um, like five or six days a week."

"So it's the thing you do together most often, other than eat, probably, right?"

Camilla only nodded.

"But it sounds like you guys might not like the same things in bed."

"How do you figure that?"

"Um, let's see. You're signing up to have sex with ten guys in one night and the guy you live with isn't here. That's my clue."

"Brad is...conservative," Camilla said, swallowing her embarrassment. For a moment she felt sympathy for her step-sister. She wondered if this was what it was like for Cynthia when Camilla had constantly brought up sex, and toys, and the right to orgasms over the years.

"So you both like onion rings, but not orgies?"

"I haven't mentioned it. Bringing Walter into the bedroom was enough."

"Oh, so you've done a threesome? Telling him about this should be easy then. I think—"

"Um. No. Not exactly. Walter is a vibrator."

"Geez, he had to warm up to toys? Okay, here's the short version. Hook up with a nice guy, who's good in bed, and gets your kinks."

"Kink? I don't like to be tied up and spanked."

"There are a whole lot of kinks, dear girl. Let me tell you that being fucked by a line of guys is a kink. A big ol' freaky-girl kink. Get Brad on board or find a guy who loves that about you. Erika and I can tell you, there's no shortage of guys who'd love to date a girl like you."

"That's it? Tell him?"

"Yeah. That's it," Angel said, pulling off her jeans and sweater. The woman had a thing for designer underwear.

She pulled back the polyester blanket and smoothed out the sheets. Plumping up the pillows, she laid herself out like a buffet. "But break it out like he won the lottery, not like it's a cancer diagnosis."

TEN

CAMILLA PULLED off the blue chintz apron when she heard Brad's feet on the stairs. The best part about a third-floor walkup is that you always knew when someone was coming.

She'd racked her brain for things someone would do when they won the lottery. Since her budget didn't extend itself to tying a red bow around a new SUV, Camilla had left work early and bought a box of cake mix.

Cake-decorating class had been super beneficial. Camilla had totally lucked into meeting a guy who craved public sex. He'd come to class to meet women. She made sure he met her in all the right places—the campus flagpole, the back of the local dive bar, and Roger Williams park. As a bonus, she'd learned to frost the hell out of a cake.

"What's the occasion?" Brad asked, his face full of alarm.

"You didn't forget my birthday or any kind of anniversary," Camilla said, trying to ease his obvious panic.

"Thank goodness. I was worried you'd suddenly turned into one of those girls who celebrate about five anniversaries a year."

"Nope. It's even better. Sit. I'll cut you a slice."

"What about dinner?" Brad asked, even as he pulled up a chair to their little Formica table.

"The best part about being an adult," Ginny started while easing a slice on to each of their plates, "is that you can eat dessert for dinner."

"Cherry almond," Brad enthused as he picked up his fork and dug in.

Before she could nibble at her own cake, she popped up. From the fridge, she pulled out a chilled highball glass of Baileys and rum. Topped with a cherry, it was called a bombshell, if memory served.

Brad devoured the first piece and was about to reach for a second when he paused.

"You never did tell me what the occasion was for this surprise."

"I want you to come with me tonight."

Brad put down the empty glass. "I can't drive."

"I had a couple before you came home. Don't worry

we'll get a rideshare. Don't worry about that. I want you to come with me tonight," she said again.

"Where?" he asked his voice wary.

"To make my wildest fantasy come true."

For a long moment, Brad looked uncertain. "It's Friday. I don't have to work tomorrow. I'm game. Where are we going?"

"You know what? Let's walk. It's only a mile away. I'll explain on the way."

"I've booked us at a place called Rapture," Camilla started.

"Rapture?"

"It's a club for sexy, open-minded couples."

"Like a bar?"

"They might serve drinks, but no, not like a bar. It's a club where people can...explore their sexual interests."

"My sexual interest is in you only. What are you hoping to find that's not already happening in our bedroom?"

"It's not like that, Brad. I love you. You really have to believe that. But I have this fantasy that I've always wanted to fulfill. I've arranged to do it tonight. I really want you there on this journey with me.

"What's this fantasy?"

"I've always wanted to..." Camilla paused. Her freak flag was still balled up and hiding in a closet. Time to hoist it up the pole. "I want to do a gangbang."

Brad stopped in the middle of the sidewalk. She nearly bumped into his very still frame. "Are you serious?"

"I like sex...a whole lot. I want to see what it would be like with a few guys...at the same time."

"Cause I'm not enough."

"Cause you're plenty. You're the hottest guy I've ever been with. I love that you want to do it every night with me. But, I'm not ashamed to say that I want more. Erika says that most boyfriends get off seeing their women fucked by other guys. Especially when they know the woman is coming home to them."

"Erika?"

"You'll meet her in a minute. She helps run Rapture."

As they walked the remaining block to the club, Camilla heard Brad's breathing change. He might not want to be, but he was getting turned on.

"Do I get you first?"

Camilla's heart sped up in happiness. He hadn't bolted. From the question, she knew he had to be considering it.

"Absolutely. First, and last. I love what you do to me."

"Let's see," he said when she steered them up the long walkway.

That was enough. It wasn't no. For now, he was still with her.

They strolled up to an imposing Victorian. There were

enough turrets and gables on the navy blue sided house to scare away a wedding cake.

"So you're going to go in there, take off your clothes, and do it with a room full of guys?"

Brad hadn't walked away yet, but Camilla was sure he was pretty close to running. He'd kept his expression carefully neutral for the short walk, but she had crossed the line he'd carefully drawn in his mind probably a hundred years ago about what was permissible and what wasn't.

Group sex was out of bounds. Maybe she could ease him into it by doing one guy at a time. It would be easier for her first time as well.

After she pressed the doorbell, an face appeared at the tiny eye-level door behind decorative iron. A few seconds later, the bolt was thrown and Erika appeared.

"Camilla! Glad you came by. This must be Brad." Erika extended her hand in greeting.

"Um. Brad, right." Her boyfriend looked at Erika's hand like she had cooties, but eventually touched his palm to hers.

"Come on in."

Camilla pulled Brad over the threshold and they entered the huge vestibule. Dark floors and darker wood paneling sucked all the light from the room. Erika opened a locker. "Phones and whatever else you don't need go in here."

"Phones?"

"They're one of the world's smallest pocket porn producers. We don't want any of our members ending up on the Net unless they want to be."

Brad handed over his phone. "Camilla?"

"I left mine at home," she answered. She peeled off her hat, shimmied from her skirt, and threw her big sweater into the locker.

"You look amazing," Brad said, nearly choking on air.

The blue-lace corset and thong had been the right choice.

"We have a room for you on the second floor. Follow me." Erika led them up creaking stairs and down a long hallway. The squeak of bedsprings and high-pitched moans escaped from under closed doors.

The room was nice. Much nicer than the generic hotel. A supply of condoms stood in a crystal bowl by the door. "Ring the bell when you're ready.

"What happens now?" Brad asked, standing by the door like he was ready to make a quick getaway.

Here's where it was going to get even more awkward. "Brad. I love you. I think our relationship is really great. I think we have something here we can build on for the future." She could hardly believe the words that were leaving her mouth. But they were true. As true as the next thing she was preparing to say.

"I love being with you. You're the best lover I've ever had. But I can no longer deny the other part of me. I really want to have more sex with more people. It's doesn't mean that I want you less. It's that I want more."

"This is unusual."

"It is and it isn't, Brad. You knew when you met me that I wasn't a virgin. Far from it. That I'd had so many lovers used to turn you on."

Her boyfriend palmed the growing erection in his jeans. "Still does."

"I don't want to give you up. But I don't want to give up on trying new things."

"You mean new dicks."

"Yeah, that."

"Is this a test?" he asked, his face screwed up in bewilderment.

Camilla sighed long and hard, trying to form the words in her brain, making sure she got this just right. It was the best chance she had to explain the inner workings of her mind to him.

"Erika said to me there are two kinds of members at this club: kinksters and the people who love them. Try this once. If it doesn't work, we'll figure out something else. But we'll figure it out together, okay?"

"Can I kiss you now?" Brad asked with a finger under the skinny satin shoulder strap of her corset.

"God yes," Camilla breathed.

The entire afternoon after she'd left the alumni office had been foreplay of sorts. From stopping at the mall to get the lingerie to baking the cake, her thoughts had been laser focused on what tonight would be like. And now that tonight was now, she was wound as tight as a spring.

Sloppy kisses moved from her mouth, to her neck, to the edge of lace cupping her tits. Not bothering to unfasten the corset, Brad licked at her nipples through the spidery fabric.

He didn't go through his usual routine, and Camilla didn't miss it. With her hands grabbing at the headboard, he took her hard and fast, not undressing her, but moving her thong aside for access. Her orgasm spurred his. Minutes later they lay panting on the bed.

"What happens now?" he asked while pulling his boxers up around his hips.

"You sit in that chair," she said, pointing to a ruby velvet wingback chair in a shadowy corner. "I pull the velvet cord." Camilla yanked at the heavy tasseled braid once, then again.

A minute later, a light knock at the door was followed by a parade of guys into the room.

For a moment, Camilla thought *what the fuck have I gotten myself into?* But Erika promised her that if she uttered the safe word—umbrella—everything would stop.

Gripping the headboard, she pulled herself up to half-sitting. The guys were hot. Erika did not disappoint. Even better than hot, they were completely nude, each one with a boner in a different stage of hardness.

My god, they were hard for *her* and the thought of fucking *her*. It was the best aphrodisiac.

The boldest guy came forward. "Rick," he whispered into her ear as he knelt on the bed. Camilla's toes curled and uncurled. She was nearly ready to come right then and Rick hadn't even laid a finger on her.

He bracketed his arms on either side of her, leaned in, and sucked nearly her whole breast into his mouth.

"Ah," Camilla said, her hips jutting in the air in surprise.

"You like that?" Rick asked.

"So much," she replied.

One second, Rick was all over her. In the next, cool air snuck across her body. She opened her eyes, and saw Rick had sat on his haunches. His gloriously hard dick jutted from his lap. He offered his two hands, and Camilla accepted them.

"Ride me," he commanded.

Oh, how she wanted to take a ride. A little taste first. She let go of his hands, then crawled to him. She grasped his member and gave him one suck, then another. Then she took the condom from his hand and smoothed on the cherry-red latex. She seated herself on him.

"Fuck yeah," she shouted as Rick filled her all the way up.

She wrapped her hands around his shoulders then rocked back and forth to get a little friction on her clit.

That feeling of riding on the edge was heaven. But Rick's jerky movements told her he wouldn't last long, so she let him put both hands on her butt and he set the pace for the ride.

Fast and hard was what she needed. Camilla leaned in. Her clit pulsated with his movements. When his shout of release came, Camilla came harder than she thought possible.

Gently, he lowered her back onto the duvet, pulled out and kissed her on the neck.

Throwing an arm over her eyes, she didn't see him leave, but heard the soft click of the bathroom door.

Camilla gave the agreed-upon cue with her hands and she heard a new man shuffle toward the bed. He lay next to her, running a hand through her hair. She opened her eyes to find a tall, massive blond next to her. Camilla wasn't small, but this guy was big—everywhere.

"Ture," he whispered in her ear, the faintest accent coming through.

"What's that?"

"Swedish. Came for college. Haven't left yet."

"Thank god you're here," she said.

"What do you like?"

"To fuck," she said.

They both laughed, then he put his mouth on hers, swallowing the laughter.

Ture grabbed her tits hard. "You like it rough?"

She had no idea if she liked it that way. Most guys treated women as if they were made of fine china. "I'd love to find out," she said.

He bit her neck, licked the spot with his tongue, then bit her again.

"Ah," she cried out.

"Good?"

"So good."

Ture took the hint and used his strong Swedish teeth on each nipple, biting and pulling until her nipples were distended and swollen hard. He took a bite on the side of her belly, leaving behind a glorious stinging sensation. Just when she didn't think she could take any more, his mouth covered her clit.

There, he was more delicate, but still he nibbled on her clit while three of his thick fingers fucked her. In seconds, she went from stimulated to orgasm. She did nothing to hold back the scream that tore from her throat.

The blond lay so his head was at the foot of the bed. Lifting her limp ragdoll body from the bed, he impaled her with his cock. She braced for the pounding by putting her feet next to his shoulders. Her hands were outside of his knees. It was the first time she'd been on top, but not in control. With one hand, he grabbed her hips and moved her at the pace he needed.

Minutes or hours later, Ture lifted up his torso,

keeping them joined. He kissed her, biting her lips, then bent his head to suckle her, gently this time.

"God, I love your tits," he said, bending down to them again. He sucked her and fucked her until he came.

When Ture had left, she heard Brad shuffle in his chair. She looked to see that he was hard a second time, his cock poking from the pinstriped boxers.

"You okay?" she asked.

"More okay than I thought. It's so fucking hot to see you on another guy's dick."

Silently, Camilla thanked the heavens her boyfriend wasn't ready to storm out. Then she beckoned the next guy.

Kinky light brown hair and green eyes were this guy's best features. But his dick was soft and he looked mortified.

"It's not that you aren't hot," he said, standing at the foot of the bed, holding his uncooperative member in his hands. "I've never done this before."

"Neither have I," she admitted. That didn't seem to improve the situation. "Why don't you follow me," she said, leading him to the bathroom.

"I forgot the rules," he said after she pushed the door halfway shut. "I'm Dane."

She kissed Dane's neck. Squeezing lotion from the bottle on the counter, she rubbed it all along Dane's pecs and arms. "You're very hard right *here*," she said.

"And here, now." He took his own hand from himself

and replaced it with hers. Up and down his shaft, she worked him until he was as hard as the towel rack pressing against her back. He slipped on a condom then lifted her so that her feet were anchored on the opposite corners of the bathtub.

"Grab the rack," he insisted.

She felt behind her head and held on to the cold metal, only realizing a second later that she was totally exposed.

"I like the view," he said one moment. The next, he'd entered her.

Dane was long and thick. He stretched her in every which direction. All she could do was hold on for dear life while he pounded her. His stamina more than made up for his earlier trepidation. Going for broke, Camilla thrust her hands into his glorious afro and took herself to another orgasm.

"Enough," Brad said when Camilla came back into the room alone. "I want you again. I want you all to myself."

A tug at the rope brought Erika upstairs and the rest of the guys left the room.

As hard as she'd ever seen him, Brad took her. First, it was doggy style. Then, they were on their sides, his front to her back. When she was again on her back, he lifted her legs and held her firm while he fucked her like he'd never done before.

Brad ground the heel of his hand into her clit, and

when she braced her feet at his shoulders, the world started to grow hazy.

"Camilla?"

"The spot...you've hit the G-spot."

"My god," Brad said, as if he'd seen the eighth wonder of the world.

When he lifted her bottom, the next thrust sent her over the edge and down a long spiral of pleasure, blotting out everything in the world except for the rainbow of colors swirling before her eyes.

Brad's second orgasm was a doozy.

When their breathing had eased and the room was quiet once again, Camilla turned toward her boyfriend. She didn't want him to leave, but couldn't blame him if this was too much.

Because as much as she thought this might fulfill her fantasy once and for all, she could think about nothing but the fact that she wanted more. Not today, or tomorrow, but a few weeks or months from now, she'd be ready for a repeat performance. For a moment she wondered if she should get a ring with more roses. She turned to Brad.

"So..." Camilla said, bracing herself for the possible letdown.

But Brad broke out in a wide smile instead. "I think I may have found my kink."

Camilla lay back grinning. This one might be a keeper.

Tabitha

Some things need no translation...

Newly divorced Portland native Tabitha Simon sets out to fulfill her life fantasies one by one. First on her list, move to France. But the language barrier makes daily life a challenge until she meets French teacher Archer Mercier. He offers to tutor Tabitha in the language of love. With Archer's help, Tabitha learns more than the French words for kiss, she finds her true passions.

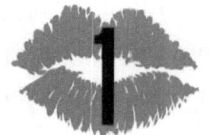

ONE

CAREFULLY so as not to get too much dust on her one remaining semi-clean outfit, Tabitha swept leaves and dust off the balcony of her new villa.

A villa.

She'd done it.

Bought herself her dream home all the way across the world in France.

Everyone back in Portland had thought she'd gone bonkers when she announced that she was uprooting her life to live her dream in France.

Tabitha gazed toward the vineyards that surrounded her house and knew one fact: she wasn't nuts. The South of France wasn't exactly Paris. She'd give them that. But her divorce settlement hadn't left nearly enough money for her much-desired studio apartment in the Latin Quarter.

Even in the *arrondissement* so far from the Notre-

Dame cathedral that she'd have an hour train ride to look out over the Seine, every single place she'd been shown had been outside of her meager budget. So with the help of the internet, she'd found her dream house in the tiny town of Clermont-l'Hérault: Population 7,395. No, wait, with her added it was now: Population 7,396.

Her villa wasn't exactly a George Clooney-style getaway in Italy. It was only slightly bigger than the studio apartment she couldn't afford in Paris. At seventy-five square meters or eight hundred square feet it was the same size her apartment in Portland had been. It wasn't a mini mansion by any means. It was much more mini than mansion. For the record "villa" is what the estate agent had called it. Not something she'd pretentiously decided upon on her own.

But the petit two-story house *was* in France if not the capital city. She had the small open plan first floor and the sleeping loft all to herself. A short walk to town on market day could get her the best wine and cheese in the world. A short taxi ride could get her to the airport and the Mediterranean Sea. It may not have been what she'd initially dreamed of, but it was nearly perfect nonetheless.

Moving the broom again, Tabitha whisked leaves from the tiles in short brisk strokes. If she moved any faster the wind would carry the dead leaves up to tangle in her own hair. It was a boy-short pixie cut, but she'd already pulled a few twigs from it and didn't want to do that again. French mirrors were all too small for detailed self scrutiny.

"Bon jour!" a voice came from below. *"Tes feuilles tombent sur ma tête."* Whatever he was saying did not sound like 'Welcome to the neighborhood.'

"I'm sorry. My French is not good."

With a huff—there was a lot of huffing in France—he switched to English.

"The leaves. You are putting them everywhere."

Dropping the broom with a clatter, Tabitha looked over the railing and down at her leaves now on a blue-plastic-covered head.

"Sorry, did I drop leaves on your head? I didn't hear you drive in."

"I didn't drive," the man said in a thick French accent. As she looked closer she could see that he was holding a racing bicycle in one half-gloved hand.

"Ah. Let me come down." In her short time in France, she'd found that Europeans preferred to talk face-to-face.

She ran to the short stairs and came down to her front door. She opened it and the man was so very close. Expensive French cologne wafted from him. It mingled with the smell of clean sweat a fragrance so intoxicating, she kind of wanted to lick it off him. Of course she resisted.

Tabitha tried breathing from her mouth to tamp down on her neglected libido. She looked away from his form-fitting clothes into his bottomless dark eyes. Like a model in a black-and-white slow-motion advertisement, he removed his helmet. Inky dark hair spilled across his forehead and neck.

She extended her hand while simultaneously shuffling back on the entryway tiles, putting some distance between them.

"I'm Tabitha Simon. Moved in this past weekend."

"*Est-ce que tu parles français?*"

"Do I speak French?" she parroted back giving herself much needed time to consider her response. Tabitha didn't answer with "no," which was on par with the truth. Instead she said what she always said. The answer that seemed to offend the French the least. "*Un peu.*" A little bit. "Enough to get bread and milk and cheese from the market." She didn't mention that she'd lived on bread, cheese, olives, and wine since she'd landed.

Eventually, she'd have to either find a way to buy the car she wouldn't have needed in Paris to drive to the supermarket in Montpellier where the shelves didn't ask too many questions. Or she'd have to learn enough French to speak with the local butcher, baker, and cheese monger. Neither one seemed likely soon. When her plan had been to move to Paris, she thought she'd have time to navigate the language situation. After all it was a city filled with foreigners. Of the seven-odd thousand people in this little town, this was the first one who had admitted to speaking English.

"I think you could use my services then," he said lifting an eyebrow so that the swash of inky color disappeared under his shaggy locks.

"What services are those?" Just his statement had sent her mind reeling to the kind of services she wished he'd offer. The kind that would have them naked and sweaty. The kind that would prove the myth of the consummate French lover wasn't that—a falsehood.

His answer of "French tutor," brought her mind back to where it belonged.

"Tutor?"

"How do you plan to learn the language?" he asked as if most people she knew didn't make do with just the one language they'd learned from birth.

"CDs. I bought a set at the airport. Online language classes. The internet has a lot of resources. It's good for more than one thing."

The minute she said that last statement, Tabitha wanted to clap both hands over here mouth. Here he was in his tight cycling clothes, with beautiful hair and an intoxicating smell and her thoughts had turned straight to naked people writhing in pleasure like those she'd watched on her computer screen.

"And what would that one thing be?" His raised eyebrow let her know that he wasn't just going to politely let the comment drop.

"Um...research. I write books. Maybe you've heard of

them. The Grunge Guides." *The Grunge Guide to Music* had been a surprise bestseller about the same time her husband had been laid off from his dot com marketing job. *The Grunge Guide to Wine* had stayed on the bestseller list for a year and intimidated the hell out of her ex. *The Grunge Guide to Beer* had ended her marriage. Even though her ex had hated those books, he'd been happy to take half her royalties in perpetuity. She shook her head clear of the bitterness that tended to gather when she remembered why she was in the Languedoc and not Paris.

"Grunge? That is something you want a guide to?" His eyes closed a moment as he appeared to be searching his memory. "Does not that mean dirt or garbage or the like?"

Languages.

Barriers.

She sighed. "Grunge" hadn't meant any of that for all of her life. Her parents had been big on the beginning of the grunge scene when she'd been born. It's what had moved them from the Portland on one coast to the other Portland on the opposite coast.

"It's colloquial." At the pucker of his lip, she explained. "It's a slang term for a certain kind of culture in the Pacific Northwest part of the United States."

"Well. Pretty lady. It was nice meeting you. Enjoy your research. *Je vais faire du vélo à la maison. Je vis juste après le lac dans la maison verte.*"

The words flowed over her ears like ocean water. Her

brain kicked in on the last words...something green. "You have a green house!" she shouted into the silence.

That eyebrow...again. "Very good, mademoiselle. Or is it madame?"

Six months ago she'd have definitely been madame. It was the word that almost popped out. The right and proper thing to say was that she was far from single and available. Older and jaded was more like it, but she didn't have the French words for that. Instead she said, "*Mademoiselle. Si vous plait.*"

"Mademoiselle Simon it is then. My house is the green one. It's just past the lake in Celles. I also said I was going to cycle home. You're welcome to visit anytime." He reached into the rear shirt pocket just above his perfect ass and retrieved a small square of paper. When he handed it over to her, she realized it wasn't paper, but a business card on thick stock. There were only four words on the front. "Archer Mercier Language Tutor." She flipped it over to see a nine-digit number separated in pairs with periods like so many did here.

"Well. Thanks for stopping by, Archer Mercier. I must get back to my unpacking."

Tabitha didn't want to be rude, but she really did want to finish getting her stuff out of boxes and sweep up the dust everywhere. She would just finish all that, have a soak in the huge tub that sat in the middle of her bedroom—an oddity she quite liked. Then she planned to wrap herself in a huge terry cloth robe, smooth on some of the expensive body cream she'd purchased from the stall next to the man who sold cheese, bread, and olives, then curl up in bed with a romantic comedy.

Her estate agent had at least made sure both cable and phone were set up. And even if the movies were in French and she couldn't find anything in English, it would be fine.

Love was love. Even if she didn't believe in it for herself anymore didn't mean she didn't enjoy watching luckier people on the small screen.

Tabitha glanced at the clock and ran upstairs. She opened her bedside drawer and tossed the card in next to that of her estate agent and the cabbie who'd dropped her from the airport. The afternoon could easily slip away before she finished what needed doing. Her goal was to get everything squared away over this weekend so she could get back to work in her research first thing Monday morning. *The Grunge Guide to Road Trips* wasn't going to write itself.

Retrieving the broom from where she'd dropped it, she went back to sweeping the small outdoor area off her bedroom. With all the dead leaves and dust gone, she stopped moving for a moment and took in her surroundings.

From the sweeping pine trees that grew tall overhead to the vineyards on all four sides of her house. Closer up she noticed that the iron work on her Juliet balcony was a work of art. Tiny pointy leaves and grapes were inter-woven with scroll work. For the first moment in a week, she didn't miss home. This, the work of European craftsmen who'd lived and died long before she was born could fill some of the empty spaces left by her ex-husband and the friends who'd chosen him over her.

Leaning the broom against the stucco, Tabitha dropped to her knees to get a better look at the corner of the iron work that appeared to be oxidizing. She didn't have any words for sandpaper or rust-proof paint, but surely with the translator on her phone she could secure it in the Leroy Merlin, she'd seen in Montpellier, France's answer to Lowe's.

It was one of the first things she was going to do as soon as she had a car, which was first on her list of things to tackle as soon as she was unpacked. Ugh, her list had a lot of items sharing the number one spot. She turned her attention back to the beautiful wrought iron, a worthy distraction from her task list.

On hands and knees, she crawled the short distance to the edge and fingered the metal. A few flakes of it crum-bled in her hands. It was nothing she couldn't...sand away was what she'd been thinking up until the entire corner gave way in a flurry of black and orange flakes. Carefully, not wanting to plunge to her death in her first week in her villa, Tabitha stood. She gripped the railing in the corner only to have it give way and land with a loud clatter on the tile one story below.

Adrenaline coursed through her veins, her heart speeding up after the fact. If she'd leaned on that just ten minutes earlier, Archer Mercier's life would have come to an abrupt end very quickly or even worse, her own. Grabbing the broom, she ran back through to her bedroom and shut the French doors tight, twisting the flimsy lock for added measure.

Crap.

What in heck was she going to do? Getting some paint and sandpaper from the home improvement store was one thing. Hiring a contractor to craft and install iron work was something altogether different. *Oui* and *non* weren't going to cover it.

Sighing deeply, Tabitha kicked off her shoes and fell backwards onto the snowy white duvet. She traced her hands along the fabric until she reached the edge of the bed. She crawled her fingers until they found the uneven antique wood of the bedside table and grasped the pull. The drawer came open with a squeak. Throwing her legs over and sitting upright, she pulled out the single business card she didn't think she'd ever need. It was time to call one Archer Mercier.

TWO

MONSIEUR MERCIER WASN'T the only one with a bicycle. A sturdy white cruiser, basket firmly installed on the handlebars had come with the villa. Tabitha had found a pump at a local gas station and had added air to the tires. The old, but well-kept vehicle is what she'd used to get her to town on market days so she could load up on wine and cheese.

After she'd washed her hands and face of the iron flakes and rust, she'd thrown her leg over the bike and ridden the same way the tutor had gone. She pedaled through town past the street that held the market, then following signs to the lake, through a series of turns onto Rue de Lac.

Within ten minutes she was at the most beautiful lake she'd ever seen. Its shimmering blue visage disappeared and reappeared as she found her way down the dusty lane that wound its way through red dirt hills where scrub brush alternated with terraced vineyards.

The road was mercifully flat, but she'd set off unprepared nonetheless. No hat, no water. Only twenty minutes into the ride, she was already hot and thirsty. For a moment Tabitha paused and considered backtracking. There was nothing behind her but dirt and land that she could see. The same was in front of her.

Well, she'd come this far, it was just as well that she figure out where Archer Mercier lived. The balcony wasn't going to fix itself. So she pedaled on. Twenty minutes later she was hugging the lake again. A cluster of houses hugged the shore a short distance beyond. They were a rainbow of pastel colors. Archer's had to be the green one in the middle. With her last bit of energy, she pushed off until she coasted to the narrow gravel path in front of the house. Parking the bike against the stucco, she walked up the two steps and knocked on the white door.

No answer.

The thought of going back home empty-handed held no appeal. She banged a little harder with the heel of her hand.

Damn.

She should have called first. It wasn't like she didn't have the phone number. There wasn't much choice but to head home to the villa. The word was mocking her all the way from the estate agent ads she'd fallen in love with.

Tabitha walked around the structure to the lake side. She leaned against the house, its stucco, having absorbed the warmth of the day's sun, was soothing. She was too tired to turn right around and pedal all the way back to her house. By now she'd been gone from her own place at least an hour—most of that pedaling. She stretched out her legs vowing to rest for a minute or twenty before she turned around and went back empty-handed.

She was imagining that movie she'd promised herself along with the crisp wine and salty cheese that she'd finally get to enjoy when Tabitha heard a splash in the water. Cocking her head to attention, she was surprised to see a Speedo-clad Archer rise from the lake, water coming off him like a seal, and sit on the dock about five feet away. If she'd thought he was hot in tight-fitting biking clothes, the skimpy black bathing suit was another thing entirely.

He looked like he'd popped from the folds of a glossy magazine. The image of her pouncing on him and licking off every single drop of liquid filled her mind expelling it of any other rational thought. Until just this moment she'd never thought of what her sex life would be like post divorce.

Now Tabitha was all hot and bothered and thinking it was definitely time to get back on the horse, so to speak. After she arranged this lesson, she'd skip the movie and figure out the best places to meet single men within biking distance of her house because suddenly she had an itch that very much needed scratching.

"Es-tu venu nager?" he asked.

"I'm sorry," Tabitha said tuning back in to her surroundings. Thoughts of hot and dirty sex with available French men had filled up the brain space she normally saved for attempts at translation. "Did you mean to call me to you?" she guessed.

"I was asking if you needed to get wet," he said. For a moment there was silence, the only sound was that of gentle waves lapping against the dock and swirling around his feet hidden by the water. At the mere use of the word wet, she suddenly was. She stood and moved closer trying surreptitiously to rub her thighs together and ease the tension building in her sex.

"I'm sorry. What?" Tabitha took a few tentative steps out onto the dock.

"Swim. Did you come to swim? Sorry. Wrong translation."

Tabitha nodded as if to accept his apology. Only she didn't think his mis translation was a mistake at all. The fire behind his dark eyes let her know, despite them probably working together in the future, that he had a frank interest in her or her body at least. The coveralls she'd been using to clean left everything to the imagination because they didn't cover much. Their convenience lay in them being easy on, easy off.

"No. I have no swim suit." Why did she say that? It wasn't lack of bathing suit that was the issue, but the fact that she'd rather be home relaxing. If it weren't for the railing she wouldn't be here.

"No matter. You look hot. Did you cycle the entire way?"

She was hot. Even though the weather hadn't been over seventy-five for days, the three hundred days of sun in Southern France could be relentless. Today had been no different.

"Yes. It was farther than I thought and dustier too."

"Come in." This invitation came from a man whose dark hair was slicked back with water. Who had droplets of water rolling down his gleaming skin. He had to know that he was irresistible. Was he married? Partnered? He had to be. She looked behind her, but the house appeared to be empty.

"Will your wife be joining us?"

"I have no wife. It's just me." She looked from the house to the man again. This had to be a gift from God or the universe or whatever was the right spiritual word du jour. She was going to take it. Montpellier singles' bars be dammed for the moment. She was going to take whatever Archer was offering right now.

Her russet-colored denim jumpsuit was a one-piece affair. She pulled the zipper from her neck past her crotch and after chucking off her Stan Smiths, kicked free of the clothing. In her bra and panties and on bare feet she walked to the end of the dock.

"Is it deep?" she asked about the water, though she was thinking about how deep he would sink into her if he made a move and she reciprocated.

His appreciation of her body was unabashed. She was getting used to that from European men. They didn't pretend not to look unlike American men who were schooled to be more subtle. His dark eyes roaming over her heated her up ten degrees hotter than she'd already been. The water would be a welcome respite from the sexual tension building between them.

"It is about three or four meters where you are standing."

No further invitation was needed. She laid one hand over another so they pointed into an arrow. Tabitha lined up her toes on the dock and executed a dive. The water was shockingly cool, but refreshing nonetheless. When she surfaced, she tread water while washing the orange road dust from her skin.

In a moment there was a muted splash and Archer came up next to her. He was so close she could see the pearls of water beaded on his long, dark lashes. His full lips had the slightest blue tinge from the cold of the water. She wanted nothing more than to press her own lips against his and see if they felt as cool as they looked.

"As you have no swimming suit, I know you did not

come for the water. Why did you come?" The straightforward question threw her for a moment. Suddenly she remembered why she'd cycled all tis way before he'd beckoned her to get half naked in the water.

"After you left. I had an accident."

"Are you okay?" he asked, concern creasing his brows. "Do you need a doctor? Perhaps you should not have taken the bicycle..."

Tabitha shook her head briskly. There was so much lost in translation.

"Not an accident exactly." she started choosing her words more carefully. "My railing. The iron that surrounded my balcony disintegrated."

"Came apart in pieces?" His question was laced with incredulousness. Despite his earlier come-ons full of double meaning, he took so much of what she said so literally. It was kind of funny.

"Yes, exactly that. The iron was rusted through. Completely rotten."

"Rotten. Only organic things can be rotten like plants or meat."

So very literal. She placed her palm against the warm cap of muscle that was his shoulder. "You understand my meaning, though, right?"

"*Oui.* Yes. I see. I am not a *forgeron.*"

"*Forgeron?*" she asked. There were so many French words. She knew so few.

"The man who works with metals to make the railing."

"Blacksmith," she clarified. He nodded vigorously.

"I did not expect you to forge iron or hammer at it on an anvil," she said. For just a moment she fantasized about his form in a bulky heatproof apron, and sleeveless shirt, strong forearm muscles bulging as he held one piece of hot metal in one hand and pounded on it with a hammer in the other. He'd make an excellent *forgeron* in her oh so humble opinion. "I simply wanted to hire you for your other services."

His eyes went impossibly darker at her request. "Other services?"

Tabitha paused for a moment trying to remember if he'd offered more than French lessons. She didn't think so, though now she was starting to hope there was more. "Language tutor," she answered finally.

"Ah, okay. Let's start now, shall we?"

Taken aback she stopped treading water and gripped hard at the soft wood of the dock, finally settling her crossed arms upon it. "I don't have a pen or paper or—"

"You do not use a pen and paper to speak with me. You only need your mouth and lips and brain to communicate with others."

"Mouth?" she asked. It wasn't that his unorthodox approach didn't make sense. It was that she'd expected to go home with a stack of workbooks, a verb conjugation homework assignment, and a meeting schedule.

"*La bouche*," he answered before he took his thumb and pushed the pad against the corner of her mouth. Her breath hitched in her throat at the intimate touch.

"Lips?" She breathed the question, her body growing warm in anticipation of his next touch.

"*Les lèvres*," he said smoothing the pad of the same thumb first against her bottom lip, then her top. Tabitha was one step from sucking that finger into her mouth and biting down. She didn't take that step, though. He was probably just being flirty. She shouldn't read too much into it.

"Brain?" she asked just to show that she was here for pure knowledge and that anything else that happened was a side benefit. The last thing she wanted was to come off as some desperate sex-starved divorcee even if that's exactly what she was.

"*Le cerveau*." His hands fitted around Tabitha's damp hair bringing her head closer to his.

These words weren't about iron work or house repairs, but she was starting to like this lesson. It was making her warm in an entirely different way from the bicycle ride. He pointed to the dock. Tabitha laid her hands on the warm wood and pulled herself up. Dripping wet, she turned so that her butt made contact with the wood. Archer did not come all the way out of the water, but braced his hands up on the dock so that she was sitting between his strong arms.

He ran a finger alongside her neck. "This is your *cou*."

The finger continued to her left shoulder. "*C'est ton épaule.*"

Despite the goose bumps on Tabitha's skin, she was as hot as Hades. Archer's finger slipped under the shoulder strap of her bra tracing down to the top slope of her breast. "*Soutien-gorge.*"

After her breath whooshed out, she repeated the odd phrase, "*Soutien-gorge?*

"I always thought *brassiere* was French."

"Canadian French." His finger hadn't left the flimsy fabric that pretended to hide her tits. His busy hand moved lower and her breath caught and held again.

"*Le sein.*"

Tabitha repeated the word that sounded like "sand" without the "d." "*Sein.*"

"*Le sein.*" His finger moved inexorably lower until it had slipped the strap from her shoulder and then her entire breast, Tabitha's *sein*, was exposed to the air. She gasped at his touch, at the cold, at the exposure of her nipple to a man she'd only met hours earlier.

"*Le mamelon,*" he said only seconds before taking her into his hot mouth. Archer teased her nipple with his lips and tongue a long moment before he let it go with a pop. "*Répète après moi. Le mamelon.*"

She swallowed a moan and did what he asked, repeated the word for nipple.

"*Le mamelon.*" Her breath hitched on the last syllable.

His hand moved down to Tabitha's exposed belly. It quivered in response.

"*Le ventre.*" He gave her belly button a tongue kiss. "*Le nombril.*"

"*Le ventre. Le nombril*," she hissed.

Those strong corded hands moved to her hips next. "*Les hanches*," he declared.

"*Les hanches*," she repeated.

A single finger moved between Tabitha's legs parting them ever so slightly before tracing a path down the satin crotch of her underwear, wet for reasons having nothing to do with her impromptu swim.

"*Le vagin.*" His hand slipped under my panties, pushing them aside. Exposing her to the air, to anyone who could see, to...him.

"*Le vagin*," she parroted on a gasp as first one of his fingers, then another slipped between her folds.

"*Le clitoris.*" His thumb landed on just that part, then didn't move.

"That's the same," Tabitha nearly shouted. She'd meant to whisper, but his thumb had moved then, the slightest bit, in a circle, abrading her sensitive flesh in a way that had her wanting to shed her own skin, peel away the layers separating them.

"*Seulement en français.* Only in French," he admonished before his mouth came forward and covered her in the most intimate of kisses. His tongue came out licking up and down, and up and down her seam until it landed and fluttered against Tabitha's clitoris. In her head the last word was said with a strong French accent, not the stuttered English she was used to. His other hand pulled down her other *soutien-gorge* strap and plucked at the other *mamelon*.

Meanwhile his mouth got busy pleasuring her while his fingers slipped deep inside until they were rubbing against the bundle of nerves hidden there. One minute Tabitha was panting Archer's name. The next her cries echoed off the stucco of the other houses along the lake.

"*Le orgasme*," he whispered into her quivering flesh.

Tabitha didn't have the capacity to repeat that one, though she'd never forget its meaning. Instead she bleated out the same "Oh my god," she always had after she'd come hard.

"*Mon dieu*," he corrected softly while readjusting her underclothes so she was half decent. "That is today's lesson. I will call you when it is time for the next."

With that he pulled himself from the lake, shook water all over the dock like he was a wet dog, then stepped into a towel she hadn't seen sitting on one of the chairs facing the lake.

Without much fanfare, Tabitha stepped back into her jumpsuit and slipped her feet into her shoes. He walked into his house with the barest backward glance, a small smile playing around his lips. Then he disappeared through the door without saying goodbye. Tabitha zipped her coveralls on, lifted the bike from the wall, threw her leg over and started pedaling.

She rode home in the twilight no closer to hiring a *forgeron*, but much closer to her newfound pleasure.

THREE

"HELLO! Are you ready for today's lesson?" The French accented English surprised her, but she nearly drenched her panties nevertheless. That first lesson had been the star of her sex dreams every night since he'd given her *le orgasme* by the lake.

Tabitha didn't dare step out on the balcony that was still desperately in need of repair. She waved from the closed French doors and mimed coming down to let Archer in.

"Bon jour."

He grasped her upper arms gently, brought Tabitha close, then leaned in to kiss her on both cheeks. He stepped back and she almost lost her footing.

He was so very handsome in that effortless way European men had. He even had a silk scarf artfully tied around his neck which on any number of American men would have looked ridiculous, but on Archer was especially attractive. Tabitha wanted nothing more than to lift the edge of that silk, pull him forward, and find out much more about how she could have *les orgasmes*.

"Hello."

He pressed a finger to her lips. *"Pas d'anglais autorisé."* Her best guess that no English was allowed. Tabitha quickly recited all the French in her head. It didn't add up to more than a jumble of numbers and about fifty random words. Probably what the average one-year-old knew.

Did he expect her to mime and gesture? She did just that, pushing the door back and gesturing for him to follow her.

"Bienvenue," he prompted.

Welcome. Right. She knew that one. Learned it from a mural in the airport that had "Welcome" scrawled in about a dozen different languages.

"Bienvenue," she acquiesced.

"Entrez, s'il-vous-plaît."

Tabitha repeated the next inviting him in. So far so good. Maybe French wouldn't be so bad. She wandered over to her tiny open kitchen with its small stove and half fridge. When she'd first seen this she had wondered how she would be able to get along with so little storage. But she'd quickly adopted the French habit of near daily shopping for her meals and was eating fresher food than she ever had. When Tabitha was done devouring the crusty bread, pate, cheese, butter, and wine, there wasn't much left to store. Any leftovers, she ate the next day.

"*Vin?*" she asked hesitantly adding a lilt to her voice so that he knew she was asking him to share wine with her.

"*Voulez-vous du vin?*" he stated and Tabitha repeated.

"*Je voudrais un verre de vin.*" He held out his hand. She was pretty sure he'd asked for a glass of wine. "*Je voudrais*" was her most used phrase to date.

"*Blanc ou...*" Damn. She had no idea the word for red. Tabitha flipped through her brain for a long second. "*Rouge! Blanc o rouge?*" She was so proud of herself for that. It was almost like she was having a conversation in French. Her very first one. All her chats with butchers or cheese and fish mongers were mostly one-sided. She asked for something. They talked a lot while wrapping her purchases in wax paper, then she tried her hardest to decipher the amount of euros they were seeking. If she could figure it out, she gave them near the exact amount.

If not, her go-to was to use a fifty euro note and pantomime that she didn't have anything smaller. Tabitha ended up with a lot of heavy coins this way.

The idea of casually chatting with them like the other shoppers made her shiver in anticipation. Maybe she could even use this French to meet men. The last encounter with Archer Mercier had woken her libido from what had felt like an eternal slumber. Iron workers, repairmen, and car dealerships had stopped being her sole priority. Sexual satisfaction had taken a starring role.

"*Avez-vous du rosé?*"

"*Rosé? Oui!*" Tabitha answered after a moment's hesitation while she did the translation in her head. She did have rosé. She pulled a small half bottle from the tiny fridge. She'd found the light pink wine refreshing in this warmer region of the country. She poured each of them a healthy glass.

"Cheers."

"*Frances!*"

"Um..." She tried to think back to see if she'd heard the celebratory word the French used when clinking glasses. Nothing came to mind. When other people were toasting around her, she'd mostly felt sad that she'd been alone. Language hadn't been on her mind. She held her glass aloft no doubt with a big blank stare on her face.

"*À votre santé!*" he finally said.

Tabitha repeated the words, clinked again, then nodded. She drank from the glass far too quickly. She could feel the alcohol rushing to her head. She had skipped breakfast this morning, choosing instead to rush through some work emails so she could clear the decks should today's lesson go...long.

"*Je veux jouer à un jeu. Ça s'appelle ce qui est. Vous me posez des questions et je vais répondre. Comme nous l'avons fait l'autre jour.*"

Tabitha finished her wine and poured herself another few ounces. She guessed that he was saying that he wanted her to ask him questions and he would answer. Her mind split between appropriate and not so aboveboard questions.

He put a finger to her lips, damp with wine. "*Qu'Est-ce que c'est?*"

What is it?

She'd seen that in a phrase book while she was on the plane. It was what she was to ask grocers about odd cheeses and the like. Although the book never said what those new to French were to do with the answers. Two could definitely play at this game.

Without the words to command him to follow her, Tabitha placed her twice empty glass on the counter and beckoned him upstairs. He finished his own wine, then followed. Her first task was the railing. She opened the not so ironically named French doors and pointed to the balcony.

"*Qu'Est-ce que c'est?*"

"*Balcon.*"

Tabitha threw back her head and laughed. Well that was easy. She should have looked that one up in her dictionary. She pointed to the railing.

"*Balustrade.*"

She had to chuckle again. Another word they used in English. She knew it was estimated that a large percentage of English words came from the French. Until now she'd had no idea how true that was. She mimed hammering and aimed an invisible blow torch at the remaining railing.

"Reparation."

He touched her lips again. Tabitha didn't resist the urge this time and sucked in the tip, giving it a nip. *"Je veux réparer mon balcon."*

I want to repair my balcony. That was easy enough. She guessed if she googled *forgeron* and *balustrade* she might find a local artisan and have this fixed in no time. She turned and pushed her flat hand against his chest gently ushering him back through the door and into her bedroom. She left the door open because she was thinking that in a few seconds they'd desperately need the cool air against their bodies.

Like she'd imagined earlier, Tabitha unknotted his scarf and slipped it from his neck. What is it she asked in French.

"Écharpe."

She unbuttoned the three solitary buttons holding the top of his short-sleeved knit shirt together. She pushed the flaps apart and kissed the chest hair revealed there. He smelled like a dream: cologne, something spicy. A real man. How she had missed the smell.

These long separation and post-divorce months had been the most sexually solitary of her life. All her friends had sworn that she needed that time to learn about herself, not make the same mistakes she'd made with her ex. She looked at Archer and his sheer presence crowded out the solitary confinement. Lightly, she tugged at the dark hairs. He shivered, his nipples hardening in pleasure under the thin fabric.

"*Les poils du torse.*"

Well that sounded way more sexy than chest hair. She worked Archer's shirt up while she touched the tip of each of his small nipples with her tongue. Her own rose in arousal when his pulled to points as sharp as tiny pencil erasers.

"I remember. *Mamelon,*" she whispered as she blew cold air on his making them even harder. Despite the fact that it has to be near eighty outside, he shivered a second time. She marveled that she was learning the signs of his arousal.

"*Je me souviens,*" he choked out.

She...she straddled him on her bed, then paused. Tabitha could not work out the rest.

He unbuttoned the Spanish peasant blouse she was wearing, spread it apart. He did the same with her front-clasping bra. "*Je me souviens de tes mamelons,*" he said while rubbing the rough pads of his thumbs across her sensitive flesh. In a flash she got it. He was saying "I remember."

It was so sexy, so hot, it was almost too much. She reared back and ground her center against his erection. She wanted him as aroused as she.

"*Ceinture*," he panted while Tabitha pulled the leather belt from the loops on his jeans.

"*Bouton*," came in gasps as she slipped one finger through the button hole and relieved at least a bit of the pressure on his cock.

"*Fermeture éclair*," came while she unzipped his denim. Cream-filled pastries painted quite the sexy picture in her head, though she was pretty sure it was the word for zipper.

His little briefs were the sexiest thing she'd ever seen. Like boxer briefs except they were super short. Just bands around his legs and ass really. It was the pouch in front that made her mouth water.

Only the French would have a cock pouch front and center. If the rest were anything like Archer, they were not at all shy about their sexuality. Tabitha scooted back and put as much of her entire mouth as she could over that cock-filled package.

"*Slip*," he exhaled in a guttural moan.

"Sexy *slip*," she said around a mouthful of cock. She hooked a finger around the *slip* and pulled it down just enough that his cock sprang free. It was as hard and thick as she'd hoped it would be.

"*Qu'Est-ce que c'est?*" she asked though there was little doubt about it. Penis was a word used worldwide.

"*La queue. Le pénis. La bite.*" He huffed each between a breath.

She cupped his balls in her palm.

"*Couilles.*"

He liked his *couilles* in her hand. Using thighs she'd toned with months of divorce-inspired Pilates, she lifted herself, pulled her thong to one side, notched him, and eased down. Tabitha was so slick that he was deep inside, filling her to the hilt in the time it took her to gasp.

"Fuuuuuck," she ground out as French escaped her completely.

"*Faire des pirouettes sur le nombril,*" he spit out between breaths.

As *le orgasme* took over, she could only hear the words like a French waterfall pass her ears. Tabitha was going to have to just assume all those words somehow meant fuck.

Archer was a greedy man. After that first go round, he was ready for a second. Her long-denied body gave in without a hint of protest.

"*Tu est prêt,*" he said two more hours later, tucking his scarf in the pocket of his jeans. "*Appelez le forgeron.*"

She was ready, he'd said. Call the ironsmith. Tabitha certainly would call and have him *réparé mon balcon.*

FOUR

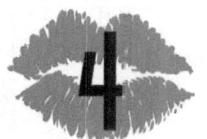

IN THE REFLECTION of her glass-smooth laptop screen, Tabitha saw movement. Shamelessly she turned around in time to see the *forgeron* stand, brush his large hands against his navy and gray coveralls, and look at the railing he'd installed making her small three-meter square of balcony safe once again.

The *forgeron* had a name. The ironsmith was called Hugo. If Hugo meant huge, and Tabitha hadn't exactly googled it, then he very much made that the best truth. For the week he'd been at her tiny villa, she'd had a chance to watch him, without looking like she was doing so.

Every day the six-foot-something man came and installed a section of railing. His strong square hands on the blowtorch were almost delicate as he made sure the joints between the amazingly rendered grape leaves and tiny fruits were strong and steady.

For those days the French doors had been open, she'd sat, back to Hugo, at her desk busily typing or pretending to type on her laptop. When she wasn't doing either, she'd angled the screen in such a way that she could most definitely see him and all his muscles at work.

On the first day, she's watched his biceps bulge when he lifted. On the second day, it was his thighs as he squatted. Today had been especially hot and he'd taken down the tops of his overalls and pulled off his shirt. Her eyes darted everywhere from the caps of his shoulders, to the traps that were strong but not bodybuilder crazy, to the lats that made his back wide and strong. Now that she thought about it, huge maybe wasn't exactly the right word. *Massive* would have been better. His shoulders were impressively wide. The taper of his dark blond happy trail, mouthwatering. The idea of touching and licking all of the above: mind-blowing.

The installation of the *balustrade* had set her a week behind on *The Grunge Guides to Road Trips*. Alas, if she'd had to do it all over again, skip a productive week of work to watch, and salivate, and fantasize, Tabitha would do it again in a heartbeat. It had been so worth it. The fantasies she'd enjoyed the last few nights had given her some spectacular *orgasmes*. Tonight wasn't shaping up to be any different. The minute he left, she was going to get in the bath with some jasmine or patchouli. Something musky and sexy to suit the mood Hugo's body had put her in.

"*Avez-vous un peintre*," the *forgeron* asked snapping her out of her fantasy foreplay. Following Archer's advice, she started with the words she knew and worked out the rest with context clues. *Avez-vous* was asking did she have something. It was her second most used phrase after *je voudrais*. Did she have a painter?

Tabitha snapped her mouth shut and turned hoping he hadn't noticed her practically drooling over the keys. Hugo had been such an improvement over the sixty-year-old man she'd expected to come do the work that she'd practically skipped for joy the minute she'd opened the door to him. Instead of gray-haired, this one was thirty if he was a day. She was never happier than at that moment that younger people were taking up the trades again. Popping up from her desk, she came to the door to talk to him.

"*Non*," she said in answer to the painter question, then paused. She wanted to ask for a recommendation. Archer had tutored her in this, as much of life in France, at least considering household matters, was done by word of mouth. Before she could spend even more time looking like a gawping fish, the phrase suddenly came to her. "*Pouvez-vous recommander quelqu'un?*"

Hugo gave a huge smile. His white teeth gleamed against skin bronzed by hours in the sun. It took everything in her power not to poke out her tongue and lap up every bead of clean sweat trickling down his muscled frame.

"*Moi?*" Hugo thrust his thumb toward his broad chest.

"You? Um. *Vous*."

"*Oui. Moi. Demain?*" He waved a hand away toward the future.

Tomorrow. It was a Sunday. God knew the French didn't really work on *le weekend*. But despite the change in geography, Tabitha was still through and through a hard-working American who didn't pay much attention to the day of the week for herself so Sunday would be as good as any other day.

"*Oui.*" She nodded for effect. Gesturing and nodding was doing a lot to fill in all the words she was still missing.

He gestured again, this time to her bathroom. "*Puis-je utiliser votre salle de bain?*"

He wanted to use the bathroom. Of course. She should have offered it earlier. If she knew more French, she probably would have. Tabitha forgot so much when she was trying so hard. She nodded again, vigorously this time as if that made up for the *faux pas* feeling like a bobblehead doll, kitsch too tacky for France to ever let cross the border.

He went into the little room that had merely a sink and toilet. Though she'd enjoyed having him around for the last few days and couldn't wait for tomorrow, her absolutely last day to ogle Hugo, Tabitha was ready for him to go. She was so turned on that she needed to do something to relieve the tension and soon—as in the-next-five-minutes soon. Damned if she'd wait for him to finish washing his hands. She could get started now.

Yanking open the wardrobe's bottom drawer, she extracted fat pillar candles and placed them around the room. With her lighter, she had them lit in no time. Next she plugged the tub and started filling it with water. Her favorite bath salt went in first so it would be dissolved by the time Hugo was nothing but a very poignant memory.

The noise of running water from the bathroom quit abruptly throwing the room into sudden silence. Dusk had quieted the birds and emptied the vineyards of the workers.

When the bathroom's folding door creaked, Tabitha couldn't help but look up. Her gasp broke the silence. In all his glory, erection pointing due north, was a very naked, very delicious-looking Hugo.

"*Je veux être avec toi.*"

Her hand flew to her mouth involuntarily. Had she been so obvious in her desire? She'd thought with her back turned and all the typing, he wouldn't have seen her crossing her legs under the desk or biting her lips when he whipped off his shirt halfway through a hot work day.

"*Voulez-vous coucher avec moi ce soir?*" she asked.

Had she just quoted the name of that song? She didn't think it was proper French, but she wanted to be understood. Lady Lavender had to be some kind of international signal. Unable to meet his eyes, she leaned over the tub and shut the taps instead.

When Hugo marched forward and lifted her like she

was no bigger than a leaf, she knew she'd achieved what any language teacher would want—she'd been understood.

She wrapped her bare legs and feet around his waist as he moved her the ten or so feet from the bath to the balcony. When they got outside, Tabitha slipped down his body like it was a pole—a big solid one of muscle.

Her hands went immediately behind her and landed on the smooth but unpainted iron railing. She grabbed on for dear life. Something told her she was going to need something solid and stable when Hugo touched her.

Without a word, he started gently untying the bows at her shoulders. The top of the dress fell into a pool at her waist. Since she hadn't been planning to leave her house, she'd gone without her *soutien-gorge* that morning. It wasn't more than a second before her breasts were revealed to his eager gaze. In each of his paw-sized hands he took a breast. She wasn't small by any means, but his hands swallowed each of her tits as if she weren't more than an A cup.

While his hands were busy squeezing her flesh and teasing the nipples that had been hard for hours, she pushed the dress and her lace panties past her hips. The fabric pooled on the tiles. Hugo knelt first on one knee, then on the other until his mouth was in perfect alignment with her—

Oh god.

Mon dieu or whatever the hell Archer had said.

Hugo's hot mouth and tongue were like magic against

her nipple. First he plumped Tabitha's flesh with his hand, then took her eraser-hard nipple between his teeth for a quick bite. Seconds later he eased away the sting with his tongue which was more arousing than soothing. The hand that was at her other breast pinched the other nipple, then slid down her side around her waist, and to the seam of her ass. She wanted to open for him but held her thighs shut to keep herself from coming too soon, too hard, and too fast.

Hugo was having none of that. His mouth left her breast with a satisfied pop and he leaned back a bit. Taking her hands in his he spread them wide wrapping the fingers of each of her hands around the railing again. His fingers then made their way around one of her ankles and slipped her right leg to the right. Then her left leg to the left. The warm evening air tickled her pubic hair and cooled the moisture that had leaked onto her thighs.

Damn.

Tabitha was close.

Her butt cheeks were in his hands one moment, and in the next his mouth was between her legs. She nearly flew off the *balcon* when she took in an entirely new meaning of French kiss. His tongue darted between her clit and her opening. She tried to hold on to the feeling, but in less than a minute she came all over his beautiful face.

One minute Tabitha was moaning and out of her mind and in the next she was being carried and laid gently in the bath. He took the natural sponge and dipped it in the warm suds, rubbing them all over her body. The sensation that was at first too much was in a few seconds making her pant with want. And what she wanted was that huge, hard cock he'd been keeping all to himself.

"*Je veux te sucer la bite,*" she pronounced.

When the head of his dick swelled and jutted toward her, there was no doubt that he understood every word she'd said.

Tabitha gathered a handful of bubbles and rubbed it on his huge cock, making it slick in her hands. The tip of it she very eagerly took between her lips. It was bigger than any she'd ever put in her mouth. There was no way she would be able to deepthroat this one, so she scooped more bubbles and added her other hand to help. With both fists and her mouth, she pleasured Hugo.

If his grunts, groans, and the French words she didn't have a hope of understanding were anything to go by, he loved what Tabitha was doing to his cock. Just as she was wondering if she could take him any deeper, he pulled away from her. In the next moment, he was lifting a leg over the tub, then the other and sinking into the scented water. Effortlessly he lifted her and in the next he'd slipped into her.

She'd never felt so full. He rocked his hips like a champ and, in a few minutes, she was screaming his name a second time. While she was as limp as three-day-old lettuce, he was still rock hard inside of her.

The minute she was able to take a breath and lift her body in the slightest, he grabbed her at her rib cage, held her still and fucked her so hard she thought she'd die of never-ending pleasure. Tabitha wrapped her arms around his neck and hung on for dear life. Water sloshed everywhere when Hugo's body jerked his release.

He fell back against one side of the tub, and Tabitha the other as she lifted herself and disengaged. No one would ever accuse this *forgeron* of not knowing what to do with his rod.

FIVE

WITH THE BALCONY complete and Tabitha's house shaping up nicely, there was only one other thing she needed. A car.

Buying a car in Portland had always been a hassle, she'd left to her husband. But she'd sold it days before boarding her flight and she needed a new one here.

There was only so much she could get by riding her bike into town or carry on the long and hot bus ride from Montpellier.

She'd been working with, and fucking, but seriously also working with Archer to get her French up to speed enough for this transaction.

When the doorbell rang, she lifted her shoulders, huffed out a breath, grabbed her bag, and walked out her door. The cab she'd prearranged last night was there. She slid into the back of the car and tried not to fidget on the ride to the car dealership.

During the last two and a half weeks Tabitha had configured about fifteen different cars online. Turns out no matter what she did, they all looked virtually the same. They were nearly all two- and four-door hatchbacks that looked nearly identical to those on the road. No matter the manufacturer there wasn't much choice in what was available within her budget.

Forty minutes later, the driver deposited her at the Renault *concessionaire*. The French word for dealership made it sound like she was off to the county fair and was going to test drive through the midway. But of course it was like any number of dealerships she'd driven past in her life. A large nondescript white building. Cars were decorated with balloons and flags that bobbed even though the air was warm and still.

She'd decided to buy from Renault mainly because it sounded exotic and French and not at all like the Toyotas she'd had for the last ten years.

Before she'd finished paying the taxi driver—it had been a case of not understanding the amount of euros—she sensed someone behind her.

"Bonjour. Julien. Julien Laurent. Et vous?"

Julien Laurent was not your typical car salesman. He was not short or paunchy or losing his hair. In fact he was the exact opposite. Tall and fit and a head full of hair that could only be described as russet. For a moment Tabitha was hugely jealous of that color. Her own was a very dark brown that she'd thought about dyeing a thousand times.

All of a sudden her palms got that itchy feeling because more than anything at the moment, she wanted to touch his hair. Resisting, she instead offered her palm. Julien at once shook, but also pulled her in for a *faire la bise,* the traditional French greeting of a kiss on each cheek. Though she knew it wasn't, the whisper of his lips against her cheek felt oddly intimate.

In the US, that definitely would have been flirting. But she knew that here, in this place of business, it was not.

"Êtes-vous à la recherche d'une nouvelle voiture?" Julien asked as he shot his cuffs. Rainbow cuff links, a series of multicolored stones set in a small square, winked in the sunlight. It made him seem a thousand times less stiff than he'd come off in the first moments. While she decided exactly how she was going to answer that question, she admired his eyes. They were lighter blue than hers, but no less warm for it. The suit, though, threw her off for a good minute.

Having lived in Portland for the last forever, men in suits hadn't been something she'd thought much about because they were as rare as fish on bicycles. She'd had to get used to men who thought flannel and corduroy were dressing up. But the smart-fitting gray suit, that highlighted his broad shoulders, narrow waist, and "bounce a quarter on it" butt was making her rethink what clothes could do for a man. Maybe they didn't have to be undressed to look good. Though naked was always in style.

"*Oui. Oui. Je voudrais essayer la...le Twingo,*" she answered stumbling over gender. The idea that objects were male or female was confounding. As far as she was concerned, beyond her own vagina, most definitely female, and cocks, the best males had to offer, learning the rest wasn't the best use of her time. But...she tried for the French's sake.

He beckoned her into the large metal building and took her international driver's license into some back room. Five minutes later he emerged with her document and a set of keys.

"*Est-ce que le rouge serait bon?*"

Usually she hated the question car salesmen asked about color. But for some reason, it was okay this time.

"*Oui. C'est ma couleur préférée.*" That was partially true. In the last months she'd thrown off the drab grays, greens, and blues of Portland for bold, bright red.

Red lipstick. Red scarves. Even red lace panties, like the ones she was wearing right now. That and her scarf. The dress was white with thin geometric shapes patterned on the fabric. It hugged her figure. and made a fabulous summer driving outfit. Too bad she wasn't in the market for a convertible.

"*Allons-y.*"

He threw the keys in the air as he led the way to a line of diagonally parked cars. The red one occupied the first slot. He tossed the keys to her.

She blooped the fob and pulled open the door. Julien was in the back with the trunk open. When he came around to the passenger side, he was without his jacket. The bone-white shirt was an excellent contrast to his honey-hued skin. Without his sport coat, she could really see his physique. He wasn't a large man by any means. She was five foot six and they could see eye to eye.

Everything he possessed fit together amazingly well though. Shoulders broader than his waist. A butt so cute she wanted to squeeze it. There wasn't a spare ounce of fat on him. She wanted in on the secret of eating all sorts of croissants, baguettes, and *tartes* and still remaining fit. A few weeks in, Tabitha realized that she'd have to ease into eating like the French before she had to buy a whole new bigger wardrobe.

Julien slipped into the small car with the ease of movement she envied about the Europeans. Trying not to feel awkward, she tossed her red scarf jauntily over her shoulder and awkwardly climbed in on the driver's side.

Tabitha took her time adjusting the mirrors and seat. She'd responsibly signed up for car insurance but didn't even want to think about the language difficulties that would be involved in making a claim if she crashed into something.

When she felt as comfortable as she could in a car that wasn't hers, Tabitha stuck the key in the ignition and shifted into first gear.

"*Pouvez-vous conduire la boite manuelle?*"

The question about a stick shift she'd expected and was able to answer smoothly almost like she was fluent.

"*Oui. Mon père m'a appris quand j'étais jeune.*" She was grateful of the fact that her father had taught her how to shift gears before she was old enough to drive. He hadn't wanted her stranded somewhere with a boy unable to drive herself home. She used to tease her dad about the fact that the stick had gone the way of the dodo in the US. He teased back that she was lucky because it was nearly all they had in Europe where they seemed to be clinging to it. They were both kind of right.

Smoothly releasing the clutch, she eased out onto the road. Driving on the main drag as she passed all the other dealerships was underwhelming. She looked to him expecting him to have her turn around at the end of the street and head back. As if reading her mind, he said instead, "*Sortons de la ville.*"

Exit the city. She was all for it and pushed her foot down a little harder on the accelerator as she shifted to fourth gear. She passed a few warehouses, a suburban tract or two, then it was all corn before they were passing open fields full of grass and wildflowers. Sure the smell of diesel had dissipated, she rolled down her window and let the fresh air blow at her hair and tug at her scarf.

At the next roundabout, she turned to Julien and he gave her a smile that made her want to drop her panties then and there. Message sent and received, he pointed through the windshield.

"*Tournez ici.*"

Tabitha followed a sign for an *Avenue de Maurin.* More green fields filled her vision. She glanced at Julien giving him her best come-hither smile. "*Ici.*" Here, he had said pointing to the right. There was a little turn-off where she could just fit the car on a small area of gravel.

"*S'il vous plaît sortez. Il y a quelque chose que je veux te montrer.*"

After turning off the ignition and pulling up the parking brake, Tabitha opened the door and plopped her Converse-covered feet on the ground. He was standing on the opposite side of the car. Even with the hot hunk of steel between them, she could feel a pull toward Julien.

Wordlessly, she walked around the hood and joined him on the other side. She stood while he opened the trunk again. This time she saw that he'd put in more than his sport coat, he'd also added a blanket. Then he did the most surprising thing, used the oddly placed handle to open the back door. Slowly he released a latch and one of the rear seats flopped forward. He moved around and did the same on the other side. Then he spread out the blanket across the bed-sized area.

"Nous devons l'essayer dans la voiture."

He wanted to try the car. Damned if that hadn't been one of her teenage fantasies that had never been fulfilled. Boys hadn't been that adventurous in high school much preferring fancy hotels on their parents' credit cards and their own beds when they could get their houses to themselves.

Tabitha didn't need any further invitation. She sat in the edge of the trunk, her legs dangling over the edge. Oh-so-slowly she lifted her bum, reaching under the folds of the dress for her panties. She lifted one leg and pulled it through the lacy opening, then did the same for the other leg. She tossed the red lace and didn't turn to see where it landed.

Julien's eyes blazed at the blatant invitation. Lifting a thigh over each shoulder, he pushed Tabitha back until her head butted the back of the front seats. Not wasting any time, he slipped his hands up her thighs and parted her legs until she was fully exposed to him. He ducked his head and without preamble took her clit between hips lips.

"Mon dieu. Bouffes moi la chatte," she said commanding him to eat her out. Not that he seemed to need any kind of invitation or direction.

Her hips nearly shot to the roof of the car with the intense caress. He pulled back and blew hot breath between her folds, then used his thumbs to part her. This time when he came back, he only used the tip of his tongue around her clit not getting close to it. When she moaned in frustration, he took her between his lips again. Julien did that intense touch, retreat, light touch, retreat again and again until she was screaming his name for anyone and everyone in the fields surrounding Montpellier to hear.

When she came back to earth, Julien was lying beside her. He hadn't taken off a stitch of clothing.

"*Veux-tu—*" She gestured toward his very obviously hard cock asking did he want...relief of some kind.

He didn't answer and instead turned toward her, lifting himself on his elbow and pushing her dress up all the way. In the same way he'd gone straight for her clit, when her tits popped out of the built-in shelf bra, he took the hard nipple into his mouth.

Magic.

His mouth had to be made of the stars or something because she usually needed a little more foreplay before a man could suck at her two most sensitive areas. But with Julien she only wanted to thank the heavens for his mouth and cry out for more.

His lips, tongue, and teeth sucked, licked, bit, and soothed first one nipple then the other. In minutes she was writhing unable to keep her hips steady. Like him, she didn't wait for an invitation. Instead she pulled away from his hot mouth and replaced her tits with her own mouth. His lips and tongue were the very definition of French kiss.

This guy had to have a graduate degree in what to do with his tongue. When she was able to clear her head enough after the initial onslaught of pleasure, she flicked upon the closure of his *ceinture*, pulled down his *fermeture éclair* and released his very hard cock from the very constraining boxers.

Tabitha turned away from him so that her hip was in the air, but her tits were pointing toward the roof. He took the hint and found her opening and pushed in hard. While Tabitha loved this position as it allowed her to look at Julien's beautiful face and eyes, she couldn't move much. In three or four thrusts, though, he found his rhythm and pounded her harder and harder with each stroke.

The car bounced, the tires crunching against the gravel, but the brake held until he came with a shudder sending her into a second pleasure spiral.

The ride back to *la concessionaire* felt much shorter than the ride out. When Julien had tucked the keys away, she'd arranged herself at his desk, hands and legs folded primly. Not a single other person in the large building would have been able to guess that they'd done a little more than a test drive.

"*Avez-vous aimé la...voiture?*" Julien asked if she liked the...car.

Tabitha nodded vigorously. She did indeed like the...car.

"Oui. Je vais l'acheter." Yes. I'll buy it.

Tabitha opened her wallet and pulled out her French checkbook and proceeded to spend the remainder of her divorce settlement.

SIX

"TOUTES NOS FELICITATIONS."

Tabitha knew better than to ask Archer what the other words were around the congratulations part of his sentence. Instead, she nodded her head in acceptance.

"Merci. J'ai acheté une nouvelle voiture." They were standing out on the hard-packed earth in front of her house. He was leaning his bicycle against the stucco fence near where her brand-new red car was parked. She kind of wanted to open the door to show him the sharp red trim on the seats. But given the way the car had been christened, she wasn't ready for a repeat performance. She'd been a bit out there lately. Not that she'd regretted anything she'd done one iota. But maybe not in the car again until it had been thoroughly shampooed.

"Je t'ai bien appris." He nodded. She had to agree, he had taught her well. Even with the distraction of sex

during some...okay, all of the lessons, she was doing much better in French than she thought she would have been able to. She wasn't exactly joking with shopkeepers, yet, but she wasn't afraid to approach them with questions. Most of the time she even understood the answers.

Tearing her eyes away from her car, she took in Archer for the first time that day. Her tutor wasn't wearing his usual skintight bicycle wear. In fact he was wearing crisp khaki shorts and a t-shirt that fitted across his broad chest.

It was almost as if he were trying to...impress her. Or maybe her reawakened sexuality was all going to her head. He probably had another appointment before or after their lesson and racing gear emblazoned with ads wasn't proper attire. She looked at him curiously and he raised his wrap-around glasses up over his hair. Dark brown eyes stared back at her.

"I am going to talk to you in English."

Tabitha could feel her shoulders relax at his declaration. It wasn't that she didn't enjoy the challenge of learning French, but it could rapidly burn through all of her brain cells leaving her mentally exhausted. Before he could speak she rushed in to get in all the words and thoughts she hadn't been able to express over the last few weeks.

"Oh my God. English. Wow. First, I totally want to thank you for your help while I've been in Southern

France. Without you I totally couldn't have navigated repairmen or even buying a car. But I've done both of those and I'm really proud of myself for accomplishing even these small tasks after my ex-husband said so often I was incompetent. That without him I'd not have been able to handle my own affairs." She shook her head clear of that mess of a marriage. She was out of it now, thank goodness. Tabitha focused on what she really wanted to say to Archer.

"I also want to thank you for warming me up. Getting me out of my no-sex hidey hole. I've felt more sexy and more alive these past few weeks than I have over the last ten years."

He nodded as if he'd expected her thanks. Tabitha could feel the heat stealing up her cheeks. Hmph. Lying naked and spread eagle in front of a man didn't embarrass her, but talking about her feelings did. Her brain was so backwards.

"It is this I want to talk about," Archer interrupted.

"What?" She waited for him to speak, not wanting to embarrass herself any further.

"I really enjoyed being with you. I'd like it to continue. But I want to be *with* you."

She was honestly shocked. Tabitha had thought what they'd shared had been exclusively platonic. The French version of hooking up. She hadn't thought of him taking it seriously. Then she hesitated. Wait. Maybe he wasn't. She was already standing in front of him and overthinking the whole thing. He was here and could clarify.

"What does that mean. Be with me?"

"I want us to see each other. Outside of the tutoring relationship. I want to have all the sex with you."

Tabitha shivered a little. She wanted "all the sex" as well. But she'd discovered something else about herself in the months she'd been here. She wanted to have "all the sex" with all the available men of Southern France.

"I want to be with you too, Archer Mercier. I want you to fuck me and teach me all the dirty French words and the not-so-dirty ones as well. But I have one request." She was proud of herself because she would never have had the strength to have been this forthright in her marriage. But that was long over and she was ready to move on just not with a single guy.

"I've discovered in these months that I have a super high libido," she started, hoping the word libido was part of his English vocabulary. "I also want to continue to be satisfied by any other man I meet who happens to strike my fancy. Would that be okay?" She was embarrassed that her voice was a little sheepish. But what she was asking for was probably a bit out of the ordinary as well.

"Is that it, little bird? Is that what was making you hesitant to accept my proposal?"

She blushed deeply but nodded.

"Oh, dear girl. Remember the day I taught you all the

words for *le divorce?* That was not just for you. I had the divorce as well. My wife, she did not want to share me. I did not want only one woman. We broke it apart before we made the mistake of adding children. I am happily single. I am also happily enjoying *le sexe* with you." He opened his arms wide in a silent plea for her understanding. "I don't at all mind sharing. It's the French way. Welcome to France!"

France, I am in you, she thought. And all of your available men will be in me.

"C'est la vie!" Tabitha shouted and threw her arms around him. The future was going to be a lot of sexy fun.

ABOUT THE AUTHOR

I write crazy, beautiful love stories because I believe story-telling is magic. I love complicated heroines with secrets, strong heroes who fall hard, and a long winding road to happily ever after. When I'm not writing, I love to travel to witness the diverse tapestry of humanity, photograph the beauty of the world, visit museums, and watch live theater. I live in West Hollywood, California ten miles from the nearest airport.

I haven't found my own happily ever after, but I'm not done trying. This year I'm going to go on fifty first dates. Join me as I try to find my Mr. Right or maybe Mr. Right Now. #50firstdates #joliemoore #crazybeautifullove

Sign up here to get weekly date updates as well as new release notifications.

joliemoore.com/50firstdates